Come What May

Lauren Brooke

Picture of Polo courtesy of Vauxhall City Farm.
For more information visit www.vauxhallcityfarm.org

Scholastic Children's Books
An imprint of Scholastic Ltd
Euston House, 24 Eversholt Street
London, NW1 1DB, UK
Registered office: Westfield Road, Southam, Warwickshire, CV47 0RA
SCHOLASTIC and associated logos are trademarks and
or registered trademarks of Scholastic Inc.
Series created by Working Partners

First published in the UK by Scholastic Ltd, 2000
This edition published 2009

Text copyright © Working Partners, 2000

ISBN 978 1407 11163 6

1 3 5 7 9 10 8 6 4 2

With special thanks to Linda Chapman

To the five grey horses who have touched my life — enriching it beyond measure

Chapter One

A chill November wind blew across the training ring, tossing Amy Fleming's light-brown hair in all directions. She hardly noticed. All her attention was focused on the black mare cantering around her. Seeing Gypsy begin to slow, Amy pitched the coiled line in the direction of the mare's hindquarters.

"Go on!" she urged.

Gypsy snorted and plunged forward again, her hooves thudding into the damp sand, the muscles rippling under her shining coat. Moving in the centre so that her shoulders stayed square to the horse's, Amy watched intently.

After two more circuits of the ring, Gypsy's inside ear flopped slightly – the point of it seeming to fix on Amy – and then her head and neck came down towards the ground, her mouth opening and closing.

Amy recognized the signal. In her own language – the language of gesture and body positioning – the mare was saying that she wanted to cooperate. Dropping the rope to her side, Amy broke eye contact and turned her shoulders sideways-on to the horse. It was time to show that she was no threat – to invite the mare to be a team with her.

Gypsy's hooves slowed down and stopped. Amy waited. There was a long pause and then she heard the plod of the mare's hooves as she began to move towards her. Amy held her breath. Suddenly the mare appeared at her side. Her soft muzzle reached out and touched Amy's shoulder.

It was join-up! Delight surged through Amy as she slowly turned and rubbed Gypsy's lowered forehead.

Join-up was a technique that Amy had learnt from her mom, Marion. By communicating with horses in their own language, a bond – based on trust and understanding – could be developed between horse and human. At Heartland, the equine sanctuary that Marion had set up to cure physically and emotionally damaged horses, join-up was the first stage of treatment. Before her death five months ago, Amy's mom had used join-up on all the horses that came to Heartland.

Amy turned away from Gypsy and walked across the ring. The mare followed. Wherever Amy went, so did the horse. Stopping at last, Amy turned towards the gate where Ty, Heartland's seventeen-year-old stable-hand, was watching.

"Well, what do you think?" she called to him, clipping the long-line on to Gypsy's halter.

"She's doing really well," Ty replied. He swung himself over the gate and came across the ring to meet her, the wind ruffling his dark hair. "She's a different horse from when she arrived," he said, patting the black mare.

Amy nodded. Five-year-old Gypsy belonged to a dressage rider called Pamela Murray. The horse had arrived at Heartland two months ago, nervous and uncooperative and with a bad habit of launching into a series of corkscrew bucks when she got excited. Working together, Amy and Ty had treated her nervousness by using aromatherapy oils and flower remedies and had then encouraged her to cooperate through join-up. Gradually Gypsy had relaxed and become less stubborn. She hadn't bucked now for over three weeks and each time Amy joined-up with her, the process seemed to occur more quickly and smoothly.

Amy looked at Gypsy nuzzling the collar of Ty's coat. "Do you think she's ready to go back to Pamela's yet?"

A frown crossed Ty's green eyes. "I'm not sure. I know she's been behaving, but I'm still not convinced that she won't try bucking again. And if she does, and manages to throw her rider, then we'll be back to square one — because she'll have learnt that bucking works."

"You're right," Amy agreed, "I feel that way too." She smiled at him, glad that their instincts were the same. Since the road accident that had killed her mom, Amy had shared all the decisions about the horses with Ty. Apart from one awful moment when she had thought he was going to leave

Heartland, they had always got on together and Amy knew that she owed him a lot. Without Ty, she doubted whether Heartland could have kept going. While he helped her treat the horses, Amy's grandpa, who owned Heartland farm, looked after the house and the land, and Lou, Amy's older sister, took care of the business side of things.

"I'll ring Pamela today," Ty said, "and explain that we need to keep Gypsy a while longer." He opened the gate and they led the mare down to her stall.

As they passed the back barn, the tall blond figure of Ben Stillman, Heartland's new stable-hand, appeared pushing a laden wheelbarrow. Seeing them, he stopped. "How did Gypsy go today?"

"Good, thanks," Amy replied.

"All six stalls in the stable block have been mucked out," Ben said efficiently. "And I've done four of the ones up here," he added, nodding towards the twelve-stall barn.

"I'll come and give you a hand with the rest," Ty said.

"Me too," Amy said, feeling slightly guilty that Ben had been the only one labouring. "I'll just sort Gypsy out."

Just then, the back door of the farmhouse opened and Lou came out. "Breakfast's ready!" she shouted.

Amy thought about the muffins, eggs and ham that would be waiting inside the house for them. "We can finish the stalls after breakfast," she said quickly to Ty and Ben, her stomach starting to rumble. Her grandpa always cooked a big breakfast for everyone at Heartland on Saturday mornings in the winter. "Come on," she said, leading Gypsy forwards. "Let's go in."

Ty fell into step beside her, but Ben stayed by the wheelbarrow. Amy glanced over her shoulder. "You coming, Ben?"

"I think I'll give it a miss," Ben said.

Amy stopped in surprise. "What? You're going to skip one of Grandpa's famous breakfasts?"

Ben shrugged. "There's loads to do still. I'll get on with the stalls." He must have seen Amy's astonished expression. "I don't mind – honestly. I'm really not that hungry." Taking hold of the handles of the wheelbarrow, he carried on up the yard towards the muck heap. "See you later," he called.

Amy looked at Ty. It wasn't the first time that week that Ben had refused to take a break.

Ty raised his eyebrows. "You heard him," he said. "We can't force him if he doesn't want to."

"But he's working so hard at the moment," Amy said, as they continued with Gypsy down the yard.

"I guess we shouldn't complain," Ty replied dryly. "Just think about what he used to be like."

Amy thought back to when Ben had first arrived at Heartland a month ago. He had been sent by his aunt, Lisa Stillman, who owned a large Arabian stud and thought training at Heartland would be beneficial for Ben. At first, he had been sceptical of the sanctuary's alternative therapies and hadn't really pitched in. However, since Ty and Amy had saved Red, Ben's beloved showjumper, from poisoning, he had started to make much more of an effort.

Almost too much, Amy thought. "It's like he thinks that he needs to work really hard to make up for the way he was at first," she said out loud, opening Gypsy's door.

"At least it gets the work done," Ty said.

"Ty!" Amy exclaimed, but she wasn't totally surprised by his comment. The atmosphere between Ty and Ben had been cool almost from the moment that Ben had arrived. And, although things had improved a little since Ben had sorted out his attitude, Amy suspected that it was going to be some time before Ty and Ben regarded each other as friends.

As Amy came out of the stall, Ty bolted the door and the two of them headed down to the old, weather-boarded farmhouse. They kicked off their boots and went into the warm kitchen. The smell of freshly brewed coffee and home-made muffins hung in the air.

Jack Bartlett, Amy and Lou's grandpa, was standing by the stove, stirring a pan of fluffy scrambled eggs. He looked up as they entered, his strong, weather-beaten face creasing into a smile. "Hungry?" he said.

"You bet!" Amy grinned.

"Can I do anything, Jack?" Ty offered.

"No, just sit down," Grandpa replied.

Lou was pouring out glasses of orange juice, her short, golden-blonde hair sticking up slightly, her pale skin flushed pink from the heat of the kitchen. "Where's Ben?" she asked.

"Still out on the yard," Amy replied. "He wanted to carry on working."

"We can't let him do that," Jack Bartlett said, a look of concern showing in his pale-blue eyes. He took the pan off the heat. "Lou, go and call him."

"No, don't," Amy said hastily to her sister. "Besides, he said he wasn't hungry." She knew how stubborn Ben could be. Having made up his mind, nothing would change it. She had a feeling that if Lou tried to persuade him it would only cause a scene.

Lou looked at Grandpa uncertainly.

He ran a hand through his thinning grey hair. "OK," he said. "But next weekend, no excuses."

Amy picked up a plate of ham. "Is this ready to be put out?" she asked, changing the subject.

Grandpa nodded, spooning the pile of eggs into a serving dish. "Right," he said. "Sit down, everyone; looks like we're just about ready to eat."

Half an hour later, the dishes in the centre of the table had been emptied and everyone's plates scraped clean. Amy put down her coffee mug and sighed contentedly. "That was a great breakfast, Grandpa," she said.

"Yeah, Jack – one of the best," Ty agreed.

Grandpa smiled. "Glad you enjoyed it."

Just then, the phone began to ring. "I'll get it," Lou said, jumping to her feet and reaching for the handset. "Hello, Heartland, how can I help you?" Her voice sounded brisk and efficient.

There was a pause. Then Amy saw a look of concern cross her sister's face.

"I see," Lou said, her voice sounding serious. "And you don't know anyone else who could help, Mr Phillips?"

Amy glanced at Ty. He raised his eyebrows. It sounded like whoever it was on the phone needed help with a horse.

"OK," Lou went on. "If you give me your number, I'll get back to you as soon as possible."

"Who was that?" Amy asked as soon as Lou had replaced the phone.

"Someone called Ray Phillips," Lou said. "His wife died recently and he wants us to take on a mare that she kept at their farm over on Wilson's Peak. She's in-foal and he doesn't know much about horses."

"Wilson's Peak? It's quite isolated over there," Jack commented.

Lou nodded. "That's why he wants to bring the mare over here. He doesn't think he can cope with the labour."

"Of course we'll take her," Amy said immediately. "Won't we, Ty?"

Ty nodded.

Grandpa frowned. "I thought all our stalls were full."

"Uh-uh. Charlie's being collected by his owner later this morning," Ty explained. "We were going to contact the next client on the waiting list but this mare sounds like she needs the stall more."

Amy turned to her sister again. "How pregnant is she?"

"Ten months," Lou replied.

"That means her foal must be due in about four weeks," Ty calculated, looking concerned. "It's not ideal for her to travel at such a late stage in her pregnancy."

"I guess Mr Phillips doesn't have much choice," Lou said.

"Will you call him back, Lou?" Amy urged. "Tell him we'll take her straight away."

"Sure," Lou said, picking up the phone.

"And ask him what she's called, how tall she is and her breed," Amy added quickly, as her sister punched in the number.

She waited impatiently while Lou spoke to Ray Phillips again.

"Well?" Amy demanded as soon as Lou hung up.

"She's called Melody," Lou said, looking at the notes she had scribbled down. "She's seven years old, a fifteen-two, liver-chestnut Quarter Horse. Mr Phillips is going to bring her over this afternoon. He's agreed to pay any veterinary fees and her feeding costs until we re-home her and the foal."

"I'm going to let Ben know," Amy said to Ty. She jumped to her feet, grabbed the two remaining muffins and folded them into a serviette. "I'll take him these."

"Do you need a hand clearing up, Jack?" Ty asked, looking round at the dirty plates.

Grandpa shook his head. "Thanks, but it's OK. You two go and get on with the yard work."

"I can't wait to meet Melody," Amy said, once she and Ty had pulled on their jackets and boots and hurried outside into the cold. "And the foal when it arrives." Her mom had rescued several mares with young foals but a foal had never actually been born at Heartland. "It's going to be so cool," she said. "Can you imagine how cute it will be?"

Ty glanced at her. "Just remember that it has to be re-homed as soon as it's old enough," he warned.

"I know," Amy said impatiently. It was one of the rules at Heartland – all horses that could be were re-homed. It was only by sticking to this rule that new horses could be rescued or cured. But just now Amy didn't want to acknowledge that – she wanted to enjoy the thought of a foal cantering around the paddocks in the spring sunshine.

Ty saw her expression. "Oh no, you're going to fall in love with it, aren't you?" he groaned.

Amy raised her eyebrows. "And you're not?"

"Me? Never!" Ty said.

Amy grinned. She knew Ty too well to be fooled by his practical words. He would adore a newborn foal as much as she would – if not more!

Just then, one of the stall doors opened in the front stable block and Ben came out. "I'll go tell him the news," Amy told Ty.

She hurried over. "Hi!" she called, holding out the parcel

of muffins. "I brought you these."

Ben unfolded the serviette. "Thanks," he said gratefully.

"We've had some news." Amy eagerly told him about Melody. "She's arriving after lunch and we're going to put her in Charlie's stall."

"Sure," Ben said, nodding. "It'll need completely cleaning out and disinfecting before Melody goes into it, and the water bucket will have to be fixed to the wall so that she doesn't knock it over when she goes into labour. No hay net either, in case the mare or her foal get tangled up in it." He stuffed the muffins in his pocket and set off up the yard.

"How do you know all this stuff?" Amy asked in surprise, as she walked alongside him.

Ben shrugged his broad shoulders. "There were always foals being born at my aunt's place."

Amy thought about Lisa Stillman's stud with its army of stable-hands and its modern barns. Ben's mom had sent him to live there when he was twelve, after she had gone through a difficult divorce with his father.

They reached the back barn. "I'll muck out the stall," Ben said.

Amy took Charlie's halter off the hook on his wall. "OK, I'm going to brush him over," she said, patting the palomino who was looking out over the door. She knew she'd miss him when he returned home. He had been sent to Heartland to have his fear of trailers cured. It was livery horses like Charlie and Gypsy, whose owners paid good money for them to be cured, that meant Heartland could afford to rescue horses who needed help and had nowhere else to go.

Tying Charlie up in the aisle, Amy began to groom him.

"Are you still planning to take Red to that indoor show in two weeks?" Amy asked Ben, as he began to fork the straw from Charlie's bed into the wheelbarrow.

"I'm hoping to," Ben replied.

He had been practising hard for the show, as it would be Red's first attempt at the High Prelim class. Six-year-old Red, whose show name was What Luck, was very talented and Amy knew that Ben dreamt of him one day becoming a Grand Prix showjumper.

"Are you going to be able to come and watch?" Ben asked her. "The class is in the afternoon. You can travel in the trailer with me if you want."

"I'd love to," Amy said eagerly. Then she thought about her best friend, Soraya Martin. "I bet Soraya would like to tag along too – if there's room?"

"Sure, that would be great." Ben nodded.

Amy smiled to herself. Soraya thought that Ben was totally cute and she'd definitely welcome the invitation. "How about your mom?" she said, knowing that Ben's mom had originally planned to attend the show but had then rung him to say she couldn't make it. "She still not coming?"

Glancing into the stall, she saw Ben's face tighten. "We haven't spoken since she cancelled," he said shortly.

Amy frowned. "How come?"

"Why should I call her?" Ben replied, scowling. "It's not like she cares."

"Ben!" Amy exclaimed, "She's your mom — of course she does."

"You're wrong. All my mom's concerned about is making it as a high-flying lawyer," Ben said, his voice suddenly bitter. "She's always been the same. When I was living over at Lisa's, she was always too busy working to bother with me."

"What? She never visited?" Amy said, shocked.

"Oh, at first she did," Ben said. "But then she came less and less." He shook his head. "I told you — she doesn't care."

Amy frowned. She couldn't believe it. Nothing Ben's aunt had told them about his past had ever suggested that his mom was more interested in her career than she was in him. "It can't be that bad," she protested.

Ben stared at her for a long time. "How would you know what it's like, Amy? You couldn't possibly understand." Swinging round, he began forking through the straw with short, sharp movements.

Amy stared at his tense back for a moment. Then she turned angrily and began to brush out Charlie's tail. *How dare he say I don't understand*, she thought furiously. *At least his mom's still around. She hasn't abandoned him — not entirely. Not in the way Daddy did*. Just thinking about her father made Amy mad. An international showjumper, he and his horse had been in a terrible accident twelve years ago that had ended his competitive career. Unable to cope, he had left

Marion to bring up Amy and Lou on her own. They hadn't seen or heard from him since. Amy had been just three years old at the time.

But that was forgetting the letter from England that she and Lou had found after their mom had died. It had been from their father. He had sent it five years ago begging for a reconciliation. Amy didn't know if her mom had replied, but nothing had ever come of the correspondence.

Just then, Ben came out of the stall. "Look," he said, awkwardly shifting from foot to foot. "I'm sorry. I had no right to go off at you like that. It's just that it's kind of a sensitive issue with me."

Amy felt her anger subside as she saw the genuine apology in his eyes. "It ... it doesn't matter," she said. "Hey, listen — do you feel like going for a ride at lunch-time?" she asked, suddenly keen to make up. "Sundance could use the exercise. We'll make sure we're back by two o'clock — when Melody's due to arrive."

"OK," Ben said gratefully. "Let's do that."

It was windy out on the trails, but neither Sundance nor Red seemed to mind. They cantered along the tracks that led across Teak's Hill, the wooded slope that rose steeply behind Heartland. Amy was pleased that Ben seemed to have dismissed the heated exchange they'd had that morning. He chatted easily about the show and about his plans for Red. When he was in a mood like this he was great fun to be around, Amy thought. She just wished she could get him to lighten up more often.

They got back to Heartland just before two o'clock. "Oh look, Scott's here," Amy said, seeing the local equine vet's battered jeep parked on the driveway.

There was no sign of Scott on the yard, so Amy put Sundance away and went down to the house. She found the vet in the kitchen, talking to Lou.

"Hey, there," he said, looking round at Amy. "Lou rang me and told me about this mare that's coming. I thought it might be best to check her over when she arrives." He grinned at Lou. "Anyway, it was a great excuse to come round."

Lou blushed and moved quickly to the sink.

Seeing her practical sister lose her usual composure, Amy smiled to herself. Lou and Scott had recently started dating.

"I think Melody's just arrived," Lou announced. "I'll go and fetch Grandpa – he's upstairs."

Amy looked out of the kitchen window. An old wooden trailer was pulling up beside Scott's jeep. She hurried outside.

A tall man in his sixties, almost bald with stooped shoulders, was getting out of the pick-up.

Amy went over. "Hi," she said. "I'm Amy Fleming."

"Ray Phillips," the man said slowly. "I've brought the mare, Melody."

He looked round in a vague manner, his eyes showing an absent look, as if part of him were elsewhere.

Just then Grandpa came out of the house with Lou and Scott.

"This is Mr Phillips," Amy said to Grandpa.

Grandpa shook hands and quickly introduced the other two.

"Thank you for agreeing to take Melody on," Ray Phillips said. "I don't know what I'd have done if you'd said no. Things have been a bit of a strain." He looked almost helplessly at Jack. "Are you married, Mr Bartlett?"

Amy saw a muscle leap in Grandpa's jaw. "My wife died of cancer over twenty years ago," he replied.

Ray Phillips shook his head. "I'm sorry."

"It was a long time ago," Grandpa said quietly, "and it gets easier."

Ray Phillips looked at the ground, seemingly in thought.

After a moment, Lou cleared her throat. "I guess we should get Melody out," she said, breaking the silence.

"Sandy – my wife – loved her so much," Ray Phillips said. He sighed and glanced up. "Somehow, I feel I'm betraying her by bringing Melody here."

"You're doing the right thing, and what your wife would have wanted," Lou said gently. "We'll take good care of her, Mr Phillips."

They were interrupted by the sound of restless hooves against the side of the trailer.

Scott went towards the ramp. "Did she travel OK?" he asked.

"She kicked out a bit," Ray Phillips replied. "She's always been nervous – more so since she's been in-foal. Sandy and I lived on our own and Melody's only ever been used to being at our farm."

"Sure." Scott started to undo the bolts on the ramp. "OK, let's get her out."

Ty and Ben came down the yard. "Here, I'll give you a hand," Ty offered, hurrying to help Scott.

"Do you want me to lead her out for you?" Amy asked Ray Phillips.

He hesitated before replying. "I don't know. It might be best if I do it. I'm not sure how she'll react to a stranger going in there with her." He stepped into the box through the side door. There was a startled snort and the sound of hooves shying to one side. "Steady now," Amy heard Mr Phillips say in a nervous voice.

Amy went to the door and glanced in cautiously. She could just make out a high chestnut head with wide, startled eyes and pricked ears.

"It's OK," she murmured instinctively, stepping closer.

The frightened horse didn't seem to hear her. She was trembling.

"OK, we're bringing the ramp down," Scott called. "Just bring her out nice and steady, Mr Phillips."

Suddenly Melody plunged backwards. Ray Phillips gave a surprised cry and the rope slipped out of his hands.

"Watch out!" Amy cried in alarm. "She's got loose!"

Dropping the ramp, Scott and Ty leapt out of the way just in time to avoid being trampled as the horse came shooting backwards out of the trailer. The surface of the ramp was old and worn and one of Melody's hind feet suddenly slipped. With a sharp whinny, she swung round. Catching sight of the whites of her frightened eyes, Amy lunged at the dangling lead-rope but she wasn't quick enough. The mare swerved and cantered straight towards Ben, her pregnant stomach swinging.

"Grab her, Ben!" Scott shouted.

Ben made a dive for the rope but the mare shied out of his reach and he fell to the ground, his fingers grasping on thin air.

With a terrified snort, Melody spun away from him. Already Ty was running round to block off the driveway, but the mare wasn't heading for the drive – she was cantering in a blind panic straight towards the nearby paddock fence.

Amy saw her stride lengthen and suddenly realized that Melody was going to try and jump the fence. "No!" she gasped in horror. The mare was heavily pregnant – she wouldn't make it!

Amy began to run but was too late. To her horror, at that moment Melody gathered herself and took off.

For a fleeting second Amy thought the horse was going to clear the fence, but the weight of her pregnant body dragged her down. Failing to make the height, she crashed into the top bar. It broke with a loud crack.

With a horrifying thud, Melody fell awkwardly to the ground.

Amy ran harder. As she closed in on the mare, her fears were confirmed – all she could see was the jagged end of the broken bar sticking deep into the horse's side.

Chapter Two

Amy flung herself down on the grass and frantically looked the mare over for signs of life. Relief washed over her. Melody was breathing hoarsely and her eyes were open.

"Quick!" Amy cried out, seeing the others approaching. She stroked Melody's warm, damp neck. "It's OK, girl," she murmured, her heart hammering at the sight of the broken piece of wood sticking out of the mare's side. "You're going to be just fine." She wished with all her heart that she could believe her own words.

Melody lifted her head and began to move her legs. "Stay still, girl," Amy said, desperately worried that if the mare tried to get up she might do herself more damage. But Melody had been disturbed by the sound of running footsteps and she struggled unsteadily to her feet, her ears flicking nervously. Amy quickly took hold of the lead-rope just as the others reached them.

"Oh my God!" Ray Phillips exclaimed. "Look at her! Look at her side!" He moved towards Melody but Ty grabbed his arm.

"Please, it's best if you stay back, sir," he said quickly.

"Too many people around her may cause her to panic," Scott explained, as he opened his veterinary bag and pulled out a pair of rubber gloves. "Hold her still, Amy," he said quietly. "I'm going to sedate her so we can see exactly what damage there is."

Amy nodded as Scott filled a syringe from a bottle and glanced over his shoulder. "I'll need some hot water."

"I'll get it," Ben offered immediately.

"How badly is she injured?" Lou asked, sounding close to tears.

"I don't know yet," Scott replied, beginning to administer the injection. He looked round. "Ty, can you give Amy a hand holding Melody? I'm only sedating her but she's still shaky and she might well go down again."

Ty quickly joined Amy at Melody's head. Their gazes met for a moment. "It'll be all right," he said to her in a quiet voice.

Amy bit her lower lip, trying to hold back her tears. She couldn't cry now. She had to be strong for Melody's sake. She stroked the mare's trembling neck and swallowed hard.

As the drug started to take effect, Melody's head hung down and her eyes began to look glazed, the lids drooping. Her legs trembled and suddenly she sank to her knees and her hindquarters thudded on to the grass. Scott pushed her over on to her good side and then crouched to examine the wound. Rivulets of blood were running over the taut skin of her belly from where the wood had pierced her side.

Amy felt sick as she thought about the foal. Was it hurt? But she knew she couldn't ask. Right now, the foal would be the last thing on Scott's mind; he would be concentrating on saving Melody. Without her, the foal stood no chance at this premature stage.

As Scott's experienced hands explored the gash, Amy glanced round at the others. The anxiety she felt was reflected in their faces. Grandpa had his arm tightly round Lou's shoulder and Ray Phillips's face was ashen with shock.

Scott continued to examine the wound, gently feeling around the sharp, splintered wood before running his hand quickly over her legs. "She's been lucky," he said looking up at last, relief in his eyes. "She doesn't seem to have broken any bones and the post has just missed her abdominal cavity. If that had been pierced then it's unlikely we could have saved her. But I think I'm going to be able to patch this up."

"So, she'll be OK?" Amy said, her hopes suddenly leaping.

Scott shook his head. "I can't say at this point. It's too early to tell. There's a possibility she'll pull through, but then she may still go into shock or into labour – and if the foal's born now it would have only the slimmest chance of survival." Before Amy could ask anything else, he opened his bag again and began to fire out rapid instructions. "Ty, I want you to monitor her pulse. Amy, stay by her head. Let me know if she shows signs of getting up and keep checking her gums. If they get pale, let me know immediately – it could mean that she's going into shock." He looked round and saw that Ben had come back with the hot water. "Ben, can you watch her hindquarters, please? I need to know straight away if she goes into labour."

There was no time for questions. Everyone did as Scott had requested. Amy crouched by Melody's head, her trembling hands gently smoothing and stroking the mare's face and cheeks. "Good girl," she murmured. "You're going to be just fine."

"OK," Scott said. "If everyone's ready, I'm going to make a start."

It was a nerve-racking time, sitting by Melody's head while Scott used a local anaesthetic in the mare's side. He eased the splintered wood gently out and then set about cleaning the wound and removing the damaged tissue. Amy alternated between checking Melody's gums and massaging her ears. Her fingers worked in small circles as she concentrated on soothing the mare and keeping her still so that Scott could get on with his work unhindered. She tried not to look at the blood-soaked timber lying to one side. As Scott began to stitch up the injury, Amy glanced at Ty and Ben – dreading that at any moment one of them would say that something was wrong. Their faces were tense but neither of them spoke.

At long last, Scott clipped the final suture and put down his scissors. "We're done," he announced. "I'll just give her a shot of antibiotics and a tetanus injection and then that's it. She can get back on her feet when she's ready."

Seeing him start to clear his things away, Lou, Grandpa and Ray Phillips came over from the fence. Their faces were full of concern.

"Is she going to be OK?" Ray Phillips asked immediately.

Scott straightened up. "I hope so," he replied, wiping a hand across his forehead. "The wound's deep but it shouldn't be life-threatening. She'll need very careful monitoring for the next week — antibiotic injections for at least two days and then powders in her food for another few days — but, providing she doesn't go into shock, I think we can say she's had a lucky escape."

Amy asked the question that she couldn't hold back any longer. "What about the foal?"

"There's still a very real danger that Melody might go into labour at any time," Scott replied. "And, like I said, if that does happen this early it's highly unlikely the foal will survive."

"Might it have been harmed by her fall?" Amy said anxiously.

Scott frowned. "It's impossible to say, but it should have been well cushioned by the amniotic fluid and the walls of the uterus. We could scan Melody to investigate but I don't want to risk upsetting her. The calmer we can keep her, the better for both of them. Just keep a very careful eye on her. If she seems in discomfort or starts sweating or pacing around her stall, that might indicate the first stages of labour." Scott looked at the mare and shook his head. "The longer she can hang on to her foal, the more likely its chances of survival."

Just then, Melody lifted her head and neck. "OK, stand back, everyone," Scott said. "It looks like she's getting up."

"Should I unclip her lead-rope?" Amy asked, as Melody rolled shakily on to her stomach.

"No, you stay with her," Scott replied. He and the others moved back. "Someone has to hold on to her in case she tries to canter off down the field. You've been talking to her for the last half hour – she may be OK with you."

Melody stretched out her front legs and, with a grunt of effort, struggled to her feet. She looked dazed and shaken. Seeing Amy, she snorted warily. Amy held out her hand. "Hey there, girl," she said.

Melody drew back, her ears flattening.

Remembering what her mom had taught her, Amy turned her shoulders sideways-on to the mare and made no attempt to approach her. Digging in her pocket, she found a couple of mints. Careful not to alarm Melody by making direct eye contact, Amy offered one on the palm of her hand.

She waited. No one else made a sound.

With a cautious snort, Melody took a step towards Amy.

There was a pause and then Amy felt the long whiskers on

Melody's muzzle tickle her hand for an instant as the mare snatched the mint and backed off again. Still Amy didn't move. Listening to the mare crunching the mint, she took the remaining one out of her pocket. She knew that, just as when she was joining-up with a horse in the ring, it was vitally important that Melody made the choice to approach her. If she walked up to the horse then she would be seen as a predator and the mare might well try to escape.

Amy took a step away and held out the last mint. Holding her breath, she listened and waited — then heard the faint thud of Melody's hooves as she walked towards Amy and took it from her hand. This time she did not move away. In two crunches the mint was gone and Melody stepped closer to Amy, her soft muzzle exploring the pockets of Amy's jacket.

Slowly Amy turned and gently stroked the mare's forehead. Melody looked at her with wary dark eyes, but she accepted the caress and didn't move away. Amy heaved a sigh of relief. The first battle in gaining the mare's trust had been won.

Melody was soon settled in Charlie's old stall. Although she seemed to be just about prepared to accept Amy near her, she was still nervous of everyone else.

"I'm sure she'll come round in time," Scott said, as he and the others looked over the stall door. "Now, I have to go — but make sure you ring me if you have any concerns. I'll drop by tomorrow morning to check her over and give her another shot of antibiotics. Keep her bed well banked-up in case she does go into labour — it'll protect her from rolling into the walls. It needs to be at least a metre high."

"We will," Amy promised.

"I can't believe all this has happened," Ray Phillips said suddenly. Amy turned to look at him and was aware that he was overcome with guilt. "I should never have tried to trailer her over here in her condition," he continued. "It's all my fault. I should have just kept her at home and managed as best I could."

"Don't blame yourself," Scott said. "You did the right thing. In another month's time the snow will have set in, and you could have found yourself with a foaling emergency on your hands and no way for a vet to get out to you. She'll have the very best care here."

"But what if the foal's injured — dead, even?" Ray Phillips said, shaking his head. "I don't know *what* Sandy would say. I've let her down."

"No you haven't," Lou said quickly. "Scott's right, Mr Phillips, you mustn't blame yourself. I'm sure your wife would understand that you were trying your best to help Melody. You couldn't have known that an accident like this would happen."

"We'll look after her really well," Amy said to him.

Ray Phillips looked at them. "You've all been very kind. Thank you." He glanced into the stall. "You will let me know how she's getting on, won't you?"

"Of course," Lou said. "We'll ring you regularly with news of her progress."

"And maybe when the foal's born you could come and visit?" Grandpa suggested, stepping forward.

Ray Phillips nodded and then swallowed. "If everything's OK, of course," he said in a low voice.

"It will be," Amy said, wanting desperately to believe it.

He took one last look at Melody. "Bye, girl," he said and then with the weight of guilt still etched into the lines of his face, he turned and walked slowly away. Grandpa and Lou followed.

"Poor guy," Scott said quietly.

Looking at Ray Phillips's bowed shoulders as the man trudged towards his pick-up, Amy nodded. What a horrible thing to have happened.

"I'll ring tonight to see how she's doing," Scott said, glancing in at the mare. "But if you've got any worries, be sure to ring me straight away."

"We will," Ty said. He walked down the yard with Scott, leaving Amy alone with Melody.

The mare stood at the back of her stall. Her chestnut coat was dull and her ribs showed through her skin. She looked like she could do with a good groom and some feeding up.

"And you need to learn to be less nervous," Amy said to her. "There's nothing to be frightened of here."

Now that the others had left the doorway, Melody stepped cautiously forwards. Her long forelock fell down over her broad, pretty face. She stretched her nose out towards Amy and blew softly down her nostrils.

Amy smiled and blew back, knowing that it was the mare's way of saying she wanted to be friends. Then she slid the bolt on the door across, slipped quietly into the warm stall and waited for Melody to come right up to her. Amy stroked the mare's rough neck and smoothed her tangled forelock with her fingers. At first the mare was cautious, her muscles tense, but as Amy's fingers moved in small light circles across her face and neck she slowly began to relax.

Very gently, Amy moved so that she could place her hand on the taut, stretched skin of Melody's belly. She glanced at Melody's face, but the mare showed no sign of objecting and so Amy let her hand rest there.

Somewhere, underneath her fingers, she knew there was a foal. She shut her eyes and tried to imagine it. What would it be like? Was it OK? Or had it been injured by the accident? Was it still alive? She felt Melody's side rise and fall with every breath. *Be all right*, she urged, *please, please be all right...*

Amy wanted to stay with Melody all afternoon but she knew that the other horses needed attention too. So after spending another half hour with the mare she went outside and began to help Ben and Ty with the chores, stopping every now and then to check on Melody.

"We need to think about getting some condition on her,"

Ty said, joining Amy at Melody's door before feed-time. "We'll have to be careful about what herbs we use because of her pregnancy, but garlic and kelp should both be safe. What do you think?"

Amy nodded. She knew that kelp would help improve the mare's skin and coat and that garlic should help combat any infection that might come from her wound. At Heartland they often treated the horses with herbs and other natural remedies. "Good idea. And we could add some Rescue Remedy to her water, too."

"Yeah," Ty agreed. "That should help her settle down and cope with the stress of being in a new place." He looked thoughtfully at the mare. "It might be best if you handle her over the next few days, Amy. She seems to have accepted you. While she's still recovering from the accident it would be good if she didn't have to cope with too many new people."

"I think so too," Amy replied. She looked at the chestnut mare, happy to take sole charge of Melody for as long as necessary.

After all the other horses had been fed and bedded down for the night and Ty and Ben had left, Amy went back to Melody's stall and began to groom her gently with a soft body brush. After an hour, the mare's coat was smoother and her mane and tail finally untangled, but Amy was still reluctant to leave her. What if something happened in the night? She sat down on an upturned bucket and watched the mare pulling peacefully at the pile of hay on the floor.

At eight o'clock, Grandpa came up to the stall. "Are you going to come in, honey?" he said, his hands buried deep in the pockets of his winter jacket. "It's getting late."

Amy looked around. "But what if she goes into labour?"

Grandpa's eyes swept over the mare. "She's not showing any signs of it." He took in Amy's reluctant face. "You can't sleep here every night until she has her foal," he said gently. "Leave her now, Amy. You can always come and check on her before you go to bed."

Knowing he was right, Amy stood up and stretched her stiff muscles. "See you later, girl," she said softly. Fastening the stall door, she followed her grandpa down to the farmhouse.

"Soraya rang," he said as they reached the back door. "I told her you'd call back."

"Thanks," Amy said, pulling off her boots. She had left a message on her best friend's answer machine that morning telling her that a new horse was arriving. "Did you tell her about Melody's accident?"

"Only briefly," Jack replied. "I said you'd fill her in on all the details."

In the kitchen, Amy picked up the phone then headed up the stairs to her bedroom. "Don't be long," Jack called after her. "Supper will be ready in ten minutes."

"OK," Amy called back, starting to dial the number. She

knew Soraya would be desperate to know all about Melody and the afternoon's events.

She was right. Soraya was bursting with questions. "What happened?" she demanded, as soon as she realized it was Amy. "Is the mare OK? Your grandpa said Scott was there and that he stitched her up... What about the foal?"

Amy sat cross-legged on her bed and explained everything.

"Scott thinks she's going to pull through but that she might still go into labour early – and we don't know if the foal's injured or not."

"Can I come and see her?" Soraya asked.

"Sure," Amy said. "Why don't you come over in the morning?"

"Great!" Soraya said. There was a tiny pause. "Will, er ... will Ben be around?" she said, her voice suddenly sounding deceptively casual.

Amy grinned. "Why?" she teased. "Aren't you coming over if he's not?"

"Of course I am!" Soraya exclaimed hotly. "I want to see Melody. It's just ... well..."

"Relax," Amy broke in, laughing. "He'll be here – he had his day off on Wednesday this week. And besides, even on his days off he seems to be here all the time; he's working really hard." She remembered about the High Prelim class. "Oh yeah, Ben's still taking Red to that show in two weeks' time and he said we could both go with him in the trailer to watch. But only if you want to, of course," she added teasingly.

"Want to?" Soraya yelled incredulously. "Just try and stop me!"

Just then, Grandpa called up the stairs. "Amy! Dinner's ready!"

"I've got to go," Amy said to Soraya.

"I'll be over at about ten tomorrow," her friend promised.

"OK," Amy said. "See you then!"

Chapter Three

Amy had trouble sleeping that night. She had checked on Melody before she went to bed and the mare had been quiet, but she still couldn't help worrying. Her dreams were full of images of the mare lying on the grass, the bar of wood sticking out of her side.

Amy woke early and glanced at her alarm clock. *Five-thirty*. It was still dark outside but she felt wide-awake and immediately anxious and so threw back the covers.

Her jeans and jumper were lying on the floor where she had left them the night before. She pulled them on, then crept down the stairs and went into the kitchen. She *had* to see how Melody was. Taking with her the flashlight from the pine dresser, she went outside.

The air was frosty but Amy hardly noticed as she ran up the dark yard. She pulled back the barn doors and went inside. Hearing the noise, several of the other horses came to their stall doors in surprise. Amy hurried past them, her heart beating fast as she reached Melody's stall. What was she going to find?

She shone the light over the door. Melody was dozing on her feet. However, as the light flashed, her eyes shot open and she started backwards in alarm. Amy hastily dropped the beam down on to the floor.

"Easy, girl," she whispered, relief rushing through her as she realized Melody was OK. "It's only me."

She switched off the flashlight. The barn plunged into sudden blackness and it was a moment before Amy's eyes started to adjust to the dark. She slid the bolts back on Melody's door and entered the warm stall. She could just make out the mare's shadowy outline.

"There's no need to be frightened," she said softly. She waited a moment and then heard the straw rustle as Melody turned and stepped cautiously towards her. Amy held out her hand and felt the mare's warm breath blow on to her palm. With a quiet snort, the horse lifted her muzzle and blew gently, her breath flickering like soft fingertips across Amy's face.

Amy stood still, letting the mare explore her skin and hair, then slowly she reached out and caressed the mare's neck.

For a long moment they stood there together, cocooned in the darkness, Amy gently stroking the mare and the mare breathing in Amy's scent. Then, with a small sigh, Melody dropped her muzzle on to Amy's shoulder and let it rest there. It was the gesture of trust that Amy had been hoping for. She gently massaged the mare's neck with small clockwise circles.

"Poor girl," she whispered, feeling the weight of the horse's muzzle become heavier as she relaxed. "Your life's changed a lot recently, hasn't it? I guess you can't understand where your owner's gone or why you've been brought here to this place. But I'll look after you, I promise, and one day we'll find someone to love you just like Mrs Phillips used to."

She leant her face against the mare's cheek. It would be so much easier if horses could understand human language. The only way that Amy could show Melody what she meant was to treat her with respect and kindness and never do anything to break the trust the mare had placed in her.

As the darkness outside slowly gave way to the dawn, Amy stayed with Melody, massaging first her neck and shoulders and then her back, hindquarters and legs. Gradually she felt the tension in the mare's muscles begin to seep away.

Amy was still engrossed in her work when at seven o'clock the sound of the barn doors being pulled back and the electric lights being switched on made her jump in surprise.

"Amy!" Ty said, seeing her look out over the stall door. "What are you doing?"

"I came to see Melody," Amy explained, yawning suddenly. "I didn't sleep too well last night."

Ty nodded understandingly and approached the stall. "How is she?"

"She seems fine," Amy said. "There's no sign of her going into labour. Her side's swollen and bruised but I guess that's not surprising."

Ty rested his arms on top of the half-door. Still not trusting anyone apart from Amy, Melody shied to the back of the stall.

"It's all right, girl, Ty's not going to hurt you," Amy said, but the horse still looked wary.

Ty's eyes swept over her wound. "How about using some comfrey ointment – it should help reduce the bruising and speed up the healing process."

Amy nodded. "What do you think we should do about exercising her? We can't turn her out in the field – she might rip out her stitches if she rolls."

"We'll see what Scott says when he calls in," Ty said.

They had just finished the feeding when Scott arrived. Amy held Melody while he examined her side. The mare flinched as the vet approached, but with Amy stroking and soothing her she submitted to being checked over – after the first few minutes, Amy felt her relax slightly.

"The wound's healing OK," Scott said as he finished his examination, having given Melody a shot of antibiotics. "Just keep it clean and make sure she doesn't rip her stitches."

"So how should we exercise her?" Amy asked, stroking Melody's dark muzzle.

"Walk her out in hand," Scott replied, packing up his bag. "She does need to move her legs or they'll fill up with fluid, but don't turn her out. You might also want to get a foaling kit ready – in a clean bucket with a lid."

"What should go in it?" Amy asked.

"Iodine, wound powder, cotton wool, a tail bandage, a towel and a feeding bottle," Scott replied, going out of the stall. "I'll bring you some milk replacer tomorrow as well, in case anything happens to her during the birth and the foal needs to be hand-fed. Also, it's probably a good idea to keep a bale of fresh straw, a fork and a muck-skip by her stall so that you've got them at hand if she goes into labour suddenly."

"I'll get that organized," Amy said tentatively, following him out.

Scott seemed to see the worry on her face. "She's doing fine, Amy," he said gently. "It could have been a lot worse."

Amy looked into his reassuring eyes. "I just want her and the foal to be all right," she said, swallowing.

Scott squeezed her arm. "We all want that," he said, looking at Melody still standing at the back of her stall, "but right now, there's nothing more we can do."

As Scott got into his jeep to leave, Soraya's mom's car came up the drive and Amy ran to meet her friend.

"How's Melody?" Soraya asked, jumping out of the car.

"She's doing OK," Amy replied. "Getting better, Scott thinks." They both waved as the vet drove off.

"See you later, honey," Mrs Martin, Soraya's mom, said, poking her head out of the car window. "I'll pick you up around four o'clock."

"Bye, Mom!" Soraya called. She and Amy walked up the yard. "So where is she? Which stall's she in?"

"She's in the back barn," Amy said. "She's a bit nervous, though."

Just then, Ben came out of Jake's stall in the front stable block. "Hi, Soraya," he called. "Amy says you're going to come and watch me and Red at the show."

"Yeah," Soraya said, nodding eagerly. "If you're sure you don't mind."

"It'll be good to have the support," Ben said.

Soraya beamed.

"How about we all go out for a ride later?" Amy suggested, eager to get Soraya and Ben together as much as possible.

"That would be great!" Soraya enthused.

Ben nodded too.

"Let's go and see if Ty wants to come as well," Amy said to Soraya.

Ty was mucking out in the back barn. "I'll give it a miss," he said when Amy suggested a trail ride. "I'll stay and work Dancer in the ring."

"Are you sure?" Amy said, not wanting him to think that they were all deserting him.

Ty nodded. "Yeah. Anyway, one of us should stay and keep an eye on Melody."

"Is this Melody?" Soraya asked, looking over a stall door.

"Yes, that's her," Amy said as she joined her friend. The chestnut mare had backed off from Soraya, but she pricked her ears as Amy let herself into the stall.

"She's lovely," Soraya said

Melody snuffled at Amy's pockets. "I haven't got anything for you," Amy told her.

"Here," Soraya offered, holding out a packet of mints.

Amy took two mints and fed them to the mare, who greedily gobbled them up. "See if she'll take one from you," Amy suggested to Soraya. "She's got to start getting used to other people."

Soraya held out a mint. Melody stretched her head forward hesitantly. "It's OK," Soraya murmured. "I won't hurt you."

The mare stepped forward and quickly took the treat. Then she stepped back, crunching the candy. Soraya offered her another. This time, Melody took a more confident step forward. She ate the mint and then nudged Soraya's hands for more.

"Come on, let's leave her now," Amy said, pleased that the mare was showing signs of accepting Soraya. "We'll come back later and take her for a walk together."

They moved quietly out of the stall.

"Scott said to get a foaling kit ready," Amy said. "Will you give me a hand getting the things together?"

"Sure," Soraya replied. "What do we need?"

Amy explained and they went down to the tack-room to collect the equipment that Scott had suggested.

"We have to keep it all together in a bucket with a lid," Amy said. "So everything stays clean."

Just then, the phone rang in the house.

"I'm just going to get that," Amy said, knowing her grandpa had gone out shopping. She ran down the yard but by the time she had reached the kitchen Lou had already picked up the receiver.

"It's Judy Stillman – Ben's mom," Lou said as Amy opened the kitchen door. "Can you get him for me?"

Amy went outside. "Ben!" she yelled. "Phone!"

Ben came down the yard. "Who is it?" he asked.

"Your mom," Amy replied.

Ben stopped dead. "Tell her I'm not here."

Amy frowned in surprise. "But she wants to speak to you."

"Well, I don't want to speak to her," Ben said. He turned abruptly and headed back up the yard.

Amy ran after him. "Ben! Wait up! You can't ignore your mom like this."

"Just watch me," Ben said, going into Red's stall and slamming the door.

Amy stopped. What could she do? She couldn't drag Ben

down to the phone and make him speak to his mom. She hesitated and then ran back down to the house. Lou had left the receiver on the table and was busily typing away at her laptop. "Where's Ben?" she said, looking up.

Amy shook her head and picked up the phone.

"Um, hi, Mrs Stillman," she said. "It's Amy here. Ben can't ... er ... come to the phone right now ... he's busy."

"You mean he's avoiding me," Judy Stillman said astutely.

"No, it's not that. He's just um ... just..." Amy stuttered.

"It's OK," Ben's mom said quietly. "You don't have to make excuses for him. I've been leaving messages on his answering machine all week and he hasn't rung me back. I've obviously done something wrong." She paused. "I don't suppose *you* know what's bothering him, do you?"

Amy felt awkward; she didn't want to interfere. "Well, I think he was kind of looking forward to seeing you at the show," she admitted.

"That horse show!" Judy Stillman sounded surprised. "I didn't realize it meant that much to him."

"It is quite an important one," Amy said. "It's Red's first time competing at High Prelim level."

"Well, thanks for letting me know," Judy Stillman said. "Look, do you mind asking him to get in touch soon?"

"No problem," Amy said. She replaced the phone in its cradle.

"What was that about?" Lou asked her in surprise. "Why didn't Ben take the call?"

43

Before Amy could answer, the back door opened and Grandpa walked in with a box of groceries. "Hi, there," he said. Putting the box down, he reached into his jacket. "There's some mail for you," he said to Lou, taking out a handful of envelopes from his pocket. "It's from England."

"From England!" The words burst from Lou, seeming to distract her from the topic of Ben.

Amy looked at her sister in surprise.

Grandpa also seemed to have noticed Lou's reaction. "Were you expecting something in particular?" he asked.

"Yes." Lou's cheeks flushed as she saw their curious glances. "But ... but it's nothing important," she added quickly.

Despite her words, when Grandpa held the letter out Lou grabbed it quickly, her eyes scanning the writing on the front. She flipped it over and read the sender's address on the back. "Oh," she said, her face falling suddenly.

"Not what you were expecting?" Jack enquired.

Lou shook her head. "It's from Joanna – a friend of mine from boarding school." Looking up, she seemed to make an effort to smile. "I haven't heard from her for ages. What a nice surprise."

Amy frowned. Try as she might to hide it, Lou was obviously disappointed. What letter *had* she been expecting?

She couldn't forget her sister's expression, and back in the tack-room she told Soraya about it. "As soon as she heard there was a letter from England, she acted real strange," she said. "Like she was expecting something important."

"Like what?" Soraya asked.

"I don't know," Amy said. Lou had lots of friends in England. After their father had left, their mom had decided to return to Virginia to live with Jack at her childhood home. She had taken Amy with her, but Lou, then aged eleven, had begged to be allowed to stay on at her English boarding school. "It didn't seem like it was just a letter she was expecting from a friend," Amy said. "It seemed like she was *really* hanging out for something to arrive."

"Maybe she's applied for a job over in England," Soraya suggested.

"She can't have!" Amy said. "She's decided to stay here."

Before their mom's death, Lou had been working in Manhattan and although it had looked for a while as if she was going to return to her city life, she had eventually changed her mind and announced that she would stay at Heartland.

Soraya nodded. "Yeah. After all, she'd have told you if she was thinking of leaving – and anyway, things seem to be going really well with her and Scott. It *has* to be something else."

Amy hoped Soraya was right. After spending most of her childhood apart from Lou, she hated the thought of her sister going to live abroad just as they were beginning to really get to know one another. She nodded. "But what could it be?"

Soraya shrugged. "Why don't you ask her?"

Amy looked doubtful. She recalled the way that Lou had reacted when Grandpa had asked her about the letter. It was apparent that she had a secret and she wasn't about to tell anyone what it was.

Soraya saw the concern on her face. "Look," she said, practically. "If it's really important you'll find out sooner or later. There's no point worrying about it now."

Amy sighed. She guessed Soraya was right, but she hated the thought of Lou keeping secrets. After everything that had happened over the last six months, she just wanted life to be uncomplicated for a while.

"Come on," said her friend, linking arms with her. "Let's go and see Melody again and take her out for that walk."

Chapter Four

On the way to Melody's stall, Amy saw Ben going into the feed-room with a pile of empty hay nets. She remembered the message from his mother.

"Ben, your mom asked if you'd give her a call back," she told him.

Ben nodded curtly and walked on.

Amy hesitated for a second and then followed. After her conversation with Judy Stillman, she was convinced that Ben's mom really wasn't as bad as he made out. "She sounded upset that you hadn't been in contact with her," she said.

Ben swung round. "So?" he said. "What do I care?"

Amy tried to keep calm. "Look, why don't you just call her? Is it really that big a deal?"

"I'll do what I want! OK?" Ben said furiously. He threw

the hay nets on the floor and marched out past her. "Stay out of it, Amy. It's my problem – not yours!"

Amy was just about to go after him when Soraya reached her. "What's going on?" she said in surprise.

Amy sighed. "Ben refuses to speak to his mom." She quickly told Soraya what had happened.

To her surprise, Soraya frowned. "Actually, Amy," she said. "Ben's probably got a point. It *is* his problem, not yours."

Amy glared at her, but Soraya met her gaze calmly.

"You think I'm interfering?" Amy said more quietly, feeling her temper begin to die down.

Soraya nodded.

"It just makes me so mad," Amy said in frustration. "You know, when I just think what happened to Mom and how I would do anything to have her still here..." Her voice trailed off.

Soraya squeezed her arm. "I know," she said. "But you can't tell Ben what to do – he has to sort things out for himself."

Amy looked at her. "I guess," she said, her voice almost a whisper. "I guess so."

Later that morning, Amy, Ben and Soraya tacked up for their ride.

"Where shall we go?" Soraya asked as they mounted. She seemed determined to be extra cheerful to make up for the tension that was still lingering between Amy and Ben.

"Over to Pine Ridge," Amy suggested. "There's some good places to canter over there, and logs to jump." She had decided to ride Gypsy, thinking that it would be a chance to take the mare out for a good long hack to see if she showed any hints of bucking again.

"Oh good!" Soraya said enthusiastically. She patted Moochie, the big bay hunter she was riding. He had been found neglected in a tiny paddock and had come to Heartland to be nursed back to health. He'd made a full recovery and was almost ready to be re-homed.

They let the horses trot along the trail that led across to Pine Ridge, the trees shielding them from the worst of the wind. As they rode, Amy felt her frustration with Ben drain away.

He, too, seemed more relaxed. Seeing a couple of fallen logs at the side of the trail, he turned in his saddle. "Shall we jump these?" he called.

"OK," Amy said. "I'll go first."

Checking that the other two were under control, she clicked her tongue and cantered Gypsy towards the two logs. The mare jumped them without a problem and pulled up calmly on the other side. "Good girl," Amy praised, patting her and turning to watch the others.

Moochie cleared the logs easily. Soraya pulled up alongside Amy and together they watched Ben. Seeing the other two horses jump had excited Red, who flung his head up and plunged forwards. Red was taking short, agitated steps and pulling at the reins. Amy watched cautiously to see what Ben would do. She knew that at one time he would have seen the horse's behaviour as a challenge – a battle that had to be won, no matter how wound up the horse became – but now he patted Red and trotted him past the logs.

"Aren't you going to jump them?" Amy asked in astonishment as he trotted towards her and Soraya.

"Yes," Ben said. "But not until he's calm."

He steered Red away from them in a large circle. The chestnut visibly started to relax, his head and neck lowering as he reached for the bit. Gathering the reins up slightly, Ben turned him towards the logs. Calm now, Red simply lengthened his stride and jumped both smoothly, his ears pricked.

"That was really good," Amy burst out, as Ben cantered up to them. Amy was relieved to see Ben was becoming a more patient rider. Red really seemed to be responding to Ben's new training methods.

"Red's a brilliant jumper," Soraya commented, as they all continued along the trail.

"I know," Ben said, stroking the chestnut's shoulder. "I'm lucky."

"He only goes so nicely because you ride him well," Amy said.

Ben shrugged. "It's nothing to do with me. He'd jump with a three-year-old on his back."

Amy knew it wasn't true. Although Red was very talented

at jumping he was also pretty sensitive and needed a rider as good as Ben to bring out the best in him. "That's not true — you should take the credit," she persisted.

Ben flushed slightly and shortened his reins. "Come on," he said, looking like he wanted to change the subject. "Let's canter."

They stayed out on the trails for almost two hours. Gypsy didn't show any signs of bucking but when Soraya asked if she was going back to her owners soon, Amy shook her head.

"She still doesn't seem quite ready," she said. She glanced at the mare's arched neck. Maybe it was the way Gypsy's muscles tensed when she was excited, or the way she snaked her head down to free the reins whenever she felt her rider relax. Whatever the reason, Amy instinctively felt that she couldn't completely trust the black mare.

When Amy, Ben and Soraya got back to Heartland they turned the three horses out in the field and helped Ty to finish off the remaining yard chores. Soraya had to leave at four o'clock but Ty and Ben stayed until all the horses had been fed and stabled, the tack was cleaned and the yard swept.

"See you tomorrow!" Amy called, as they finally got into their pick-ups to go home.

"See you!" Ty shouted back. "Don't stay up with Melody all night."

Amy grinned. Sometimes Ty seemed to know her too well!

She waved them off, then collected a grooming bucket from the tack-room and went up to Melody's stall. The mare was looking over her door. She pricked her ears when she saw Amy and, for the first time since she had arrived at Heartland, whinnied a greeting.

"Hi, Melody," Amy said, delighted that the mare seemed so pleased to see her.

She stroked Melody's nose, then tied her up and began the grooming. As she brushed and curried, Amy let her mind go blank. She didn't think about Lou and the mystery letter she was waiting for, she didn't think about Ben and his problems, she just concentrated on rhythmically sweeping the brush across Melody's dull coat until a faint shine began to emerge.

At last, Amy paused and wiped the back of one hand across her hot, dusty forehead. "You're a good girl," she murmured. "I'll ring Mr Phillips tonight and tell him how you're doing."

She pulled the brush across the curry comb to clean its bristles of dirt and grease. But as she stepped towards Melody again, she froze. The mare's side seemed to jerk. Amy stared. There! It happened again! A definite movement!

Amy's heart somersaulted. She dropped the brush and put her hand against Melody's side. This time she felt as well as saw it. A kicking movement! A kicking so strong that the shape of a small hoof could almost be seen through Melody's coat. It was the foal! It must be alive!

"Oh, Melody," Amy whispered in delight.

Melody snorted softly. She seemed completely unconcerned about the kicking. Amy undid Melody's halter, quickly kissed her nose and ran out of the stall. She had to tell Grandpa and Lou!

She raced down the yard, her heart banging. It was the first sign they'd had that the foal was alive. She couldn't wait to share the news.

She kicked off her boots and ran into the house. A casserole was bubbling on the kitchen stove but the kitchen was empty. Suddenly Amy heard the sound of Lou and Grandpa talking in the hall. She hurried towards the connecting door but as she reached it, her grandpa's words stopped her in her tracks.

"And you haven't told Amy?"

Amy paused, her hand hovering over the door handle. *Told me what?* she thought.

She heard her sister's voice. "Only Scott knows. I didn't want to say anything until I got a reply, Grandpa. I didn't want to get Amy's hopes up. It's been so awful waiting … knowing each day that there could be a letter."

A letter! Amy felt her spine tingle. Lou had to be talking about the letter she had been waiting for from England. *But what's it got to do with me?* she wondered.

"Lou, you have to be straight with her," Grandpa said, and Amy noticed an intense note in his voice that she had never heard before. "You should have told her before you wrote in the first place."

"But what if he doesn't write back?" Lou said.

"Amy still has the right to know. You can't..."

It was too much. "I've got the right to know what?" Amy said, opening the door.

Grandpa and Lou swung round.

"Amy!" Lou exclaimed, shocked.

"How long have you been there?" Grandpa said quickly.

Amy didn't answer him. She was staring at Lou. "What should you have told me, Lou?" she demanded.

Lou looked desperately at Grandpa. "I ... well..." she stammered.

"What is it?" Amy cried, feeling increasingly alarmed. "Lou? *Who* have you written to?"

Lou took a breath. "Daddy," she said.

For a moment, Amy was too shocked to speak. *Daddy!* She stared at Lou. Somehow she had known that was the answer, but she was still caught off guard.

"I wrote to him after we found the letter in Mom's room." The words came out in a rush. "I sent it to the address on the back of the envelope in the hope that he still lives there. I told him about Mom and that ... that we wanted to see him."

"*See* him!" Amy exclaimed, finding her voice at last. She stepped backwards. "You must be kidding!"

She felt as if her world was falling down around her. All her life, her father had been a distant, shadowy figure. Sure, she had sometimes felt curious about him, wondered what he looked like, whether she was like him — but she had never wanted to *meet* him. He had abandoned them and although she could not remember him, she could remember the nights when her mom had cried as if she were never going to stop, when nothing and no one had been able to comfort her. Mom had recovered in the end, moved on, founded Heartland. But Amy had always known that the sadness from that time had never left her; it had just been pushed way under the surface.

She shook her head. "I don't want to see him! I won't!"

"But he's our father," Lou exclaimed.

"So?" Amy cried. "He abandoned us!"

"He tried to make things right!" Lou protested. "You saw the letter, Amy. He asked Mom for a reconciliation."

"I don't care!" Amy shouted.

"Amy, calm down," Jack Bartlett said, stepping towards her. "We don't even know if he's received the letter. It's five years since he wrote to your mom. That address is probably an old one."

Amy looked at him desperately. "But what if it isn't?" she exclaimed. "Grandpa, what if he writes back and wants to come here?" Her eyes frantically searched his face. Surely Grandpa didn't want Daddy to come to Heartland. "Think of what he did to Mom — to us!"

A shadow crossed Jack's eyes. "I..." His voice trailed off and in that moment, in the look she saw cross his face, Amy knew she was right.

Lou must also have seen the expression in their grandpa's eyes. "Grandpa!" she exclaimed, horrified.

"Lou..." Jack began but then he broke off again, shaking his head. "Look, let's not argue, we can discuss it more when — *if* — your father gets in touch."

"He will!" Lou said. "I just know it!"

"Honey, don't get your hopes up too high," Jack said wearily. "After all, he's always known the address here and even if your mom hadn't wanted to see him, he could have got in touch with you at any time."

"But maybe he was worried about how Mom would react," Lou said. "Now he's got my letter he *knows* that we want to see him."

Amy felt indignant. "*You* want to," she said. "Don't go making promises for me, Lou."

Lou turned on her, her eyes flashing with exasperation. "Amy!"

"No more arguing!" Jack held up his hands and looked at them both. "*Please*."

Amy saw the tension around his mouth and eyes and bit back the angry words that were springing to her lips. It couldn't be easy for Grandpa. He had always tried to be neutral about their father when he came up in conversation, but she now realized how hard this must have been for him. He'd been the one who had helped her mom slowly piece her life back together after the break-up. Arguing with Lou would only upset him even more.

Amy stared mutinously at her sister but didn't say another word.

"Thank you," Jack said quietly. "Now, can we just agree to leave this alone for the time being?"

Amy and Lou stared at each other, the silence between them weighted with anger. But Lou seemed as reluctant as Amy to upset Grandpa further. She nodded. "OK," she said.

Amy nodded too and saw the evident relief on Grandpa's face. "I'm going to get changed," she muttered, heading for the staircase. Right now, she just wanted to be alone.

In her room, she sat down on the bed. Her thoughts were whirling and it was only now that she remembered she had meant to tell Grandpa and Lou about Melody's foal kicking. Right this moment, even *that* didn't seem important. How could Lou have written to their father without discussing it with her first?

But then, deep inside, Amy knew how. Her mom had often told her about the special bond that Lou and Daddy had seemed to have. She had said how similar they were – both practical, brave and determined – and Amy had seen the photographs that her mom had kept of the two of them riding together. How must Lou have felt when Daddy abandoned them?

Thinking about the photographs, Amy opened her bedside drawer and rummaged around until she found a photo that she kept in there. It was one of all four of them – her, Lou, Mom and Daddy – sitting on a beach beside an enormous sandcastle. They were all smiling. She looked at herself — a skinny two-year-old with straight, dark-blonde hair, standing by Mom. Daddy had his arm round Lou's shoulders.

Amy studied her father's features and then took the photograph over to the mirror. She looked more like him than her mom. They had the same thickly-lashed grey eyes, the same high, wide cheekbones and determined mouths. And yet she didn't know him at all. She shared the same looks with him but they were strangers.

She looked at the photograph again. "I don't want to see you," she whispered fiercely.

But despite her words, Amy knew that deep down inside her — in a hidden corner of her heart — she desperately longed to know what her father was like.

Chapter Five

When Amy opened her eyes the next morning, she lay in bed for a moment with the feeling that she had just woken from a horrible nightmare. Then everything came flooding back. It wasn't a nightmare; it was real. Lou had written to Daddy. He might write back. He might even arrange to visit.

Well, I won't be here, Amy thought, hurriedly pushing back the covers and getting out of bed. *I'm not seeing him. I don't care what Lou says.*

She got dressed quickly, wanting to get out of the house before either Lou or Grandpa got up. Dinner the night before had been strained. She and Lou had hardly spoken a word to one another and Grandpa had been quiet, lost in his own thoughts.

As Amy got the morning feeds ready, she heard the sound

of a car drawing up outside the house. She looked out of the feed-room and saw Ben getting out of his smart black pick-up. "You're early," she called in surprise. She glanced at her watch. It was only six-thirty – an hour before Ben officially started work.

Ben shrugged. "It's always more of a rush to get things done on the days you're at school. I knew it would help if I got started now."

He was right but, even so, Amy didn't want him to feel obliged to work such long days. "We can manage," she said, seeing shadows of tiredness under his eyes. "You don't have to put in all these extra hours."

"It's no problem," Ben said, coming into the feed-room. "Now, what do you want me to do first? The hay nets?"

Amy nodded. There was no point arguing – if he wanted to work so hard then she wasn't going to stop him.

Ben picked up the pile of empty hay nets and took them to the small hay-store that had been built on to the side of the stone feed-room. Every few days the hay-store was filled up with bales from the big barn behind the tack-room. Grandpa had built it so that full hay nets didn't have to be lugged all the way from the barn twice a day. Amy heard the sound of Ben shaking up the compact flakes of hay. "How's Melody this morning?" he called.

With a start, Amy stopped mixing up the feeds. Of course! The news about the foal! She rushed round to the hay-store. "Her foal's definitely alive!" she said. She quickly told Ben all about seeing and feeling the kicking movement in Melody's side.

"That's brilliant," Ben said, straightening up immediately. "They normally start kicking a couple of weeks before they're born. Jack and Lou must be relieved."

Amy hesitated. "They don't know yet," she admitted.

Ben looked at her in astonishment. "You haven't told them?"

Amy shook her head. "We had a bit of an argument last night," she said, realizing that she needed to give him some sort of explanation. "It kind of spoilt the moment." She didn't want to say any more and she turned hastily. "I'll go and give the horses their feeds," she said, grabbing a pile of feed buckets and striding out into the yard.

To Amy's relief, Ben didn't ask for any more details. They fed and watered the horses and then, leaving him to start on the stalls, Amy went inside to get ready for school.

Back downstairs after taking a shower, she found Lou sitting at the kitchen table, reading the papers over a cup of coffee. Hearing the sound of footsteps, Lou looked up, but then saw it was Amy and immediately looked down again.

Ignoring her sister, Amy fetched a bowl and shook out some breakfast cereal from a packet. She sat down at the far end of the table and ate it quickly. Neither of them spoke.

Just as Amy was finishing, Grandpa came into the kitchen. "Morning," he said. The two girls looked up.

"Hi, Grandpa," Amy said, getting up to put her empty bowl in the sink. "Do you want a coffee?"

Jack nodded. "Thanks."

Amy poured him a cup and was about to tell him about Melody's foal when the back door burst open. Ty stood in the porch. "Ben's just told me the news about Melody's foal!" he said, looking delighted. "Isn't it great!"

Amy saw Grandpa and Lou look at Ty in confusion.

"What news?" Grandpa said blankly.

"About the foal kicking!" Ty said in surprise. He turned quickly to Amy, a frown crossing his face. "Ben has got it right, hasn't he? He said you saw it last night."

Amy felt herself start to go red. "Yeah, I did," she admitted.

"But that's fantastic!" Lou exclaimed, getting to her feet. "It must be a real survivor after that fall."

"Why didn't you tell us?" Grandpa said to Amy.

"I was just about to," Amy said. She grabbed her school-bag off the floor, not wanting to look at their astonished faces any more. "I'm going to school," she said.

"Amy…" Grandpa began, but Amy didn't stop.

"I'll be late. See you this afternoon," she said, running out of the house

Ty followed her. "What's going on?" he asked, catching up with her.

Amy paused for a moment. "It's a long story," she said, her eyes begging him not to question her. "I'll … I'll tell you this evening." Shifting her rucksack on to her shoulder, she set off down the drive.

"See you later," Ty called.

Amy nodded but didn't look back. She knew she'd have to explain things to him later, but right at this minute she didn't feel like talking about the night before – not to Ty or even to Soraya.

"You're quiet today," Soraya said, when the bus reached school. "Are you OK?"

"Yeah, fine," Amy said quickly.

Soraya didn't look convinced. "Are you sure?"

"Yes!" Amy insisted.

Soraya held her gaze for a moment but then, to Amy's relief, seemingly decided not to press the matter further.

Amy couldn't concentrate at all that day. Every time a teacher started talking, she drifted off into her own thoughts. Had the mail arrived at home? Maybe even now Lou was opening a letter from their father. Maybe, somewhere in England, he was reading Lou's letter – or, at this moment, he was sitting down and writing a reply.

Amy could tell that Soraya had sensed something was up. Best friends since third grade, they knew each other inside out. On the way home on the bus that afternoon, Amy finally gave up trying to pretend that nothing was the matter and told her everything.

Soraya's eyes widened. "Lou's written to your father!" She

spoke in a low voice so that no one else could hear, but her face showed her shock. "When?"

"About six weeks ago," Amy said. "She's been waiting for a reply."

Soraya's eyes scanned Amy's face. "But what are you going to do if he does get in touch?"

"I don't know," Amy said, pushing a hand through her hair. "Lou wants to meet him of course but..." Her voice trailed off.

"You don't?" Soraya said, finishing the thought for her.

Amy saw the understanding in her friend's dark-brown eyes. "No," she said, shaking her head. "I don't *ever* want to see him." She spoke the words as if trying to convince herself of the truth of what she was saying.

"What about your grandpa?" Soraya asked. "What's he said?"

"Just that we should wait and see if Daddy gets in touch," Amy replied. She remembered the look that had crossed his face the night before. "But he can say what he likes – I *know* he doesn't want Daddy at Heartland." Her voice rose slightly. "I just don't get how Lou can be so selfish! Surely she knows that Grandpa wouldn't want to see Daddy? I mean, he was the one who had to look after Mom after Daddy left us." Distant memories flooded her mind – Mom crying endlessly in her bedroom at Heartland, Grandpa trying to comfort her. "What's Lou on?" she demanded.

Soraya hesitated. "Well, I guess she must still love your father."

"How can she?" Amy exploded. Suddenly realizing that several kids nearby had turned to look at them both, she dropped her voice again. "I hate him," she hissed. The back of her eyes felt hot. "I'll never forgive him for what he did to Mom. *Never!*" Her eyes blurred and she looked quickly down at her knees and angrily blinked back her tears.

Soraya reached out and squeezed her hand.

Amy continued to stare at her knees. *I mean it*, she thought. *I hate him and I'll never forgive him!*

When Amy got off the school bus she went straight up to Melody's stall. She wanted to push all thoughts about her father to the back of her mind. "Hello, girl," she murmured, as Melody gave a welcoming whicker. "Have you missed me?"

Melody nuzzled her shoulder in reply.

"She seems to be settling down a bit." A voice came from behind her, and Amy turned around. It was Ty. He came out of a nearby stall.

"I've been in with her a few times today," he said. "And I think she's beginning to get used to me." He came over to the door and offered his palm for Melody to sniff. The mare cautiously stretched her muzzle forward and blew in and out.

"That's a big improvement," Amy said in surprise. "A few days ago she wouldn't have come anywhere near you."

"We could take her out for a walk together," Ty suggested.

Amy nodded. "I'll just get changed."

She ran down to the house and quickly pulled on her old jeans and jumper.

"Let's walk down the drive," Amy said, joining Ty by Melody's stall.

At first, Melody's ears flickered backwards uneasily and she kept looking at Ty warily as he walked beside Amy down the drive, but after a few minutes she seemed to start relaxing.

"Have you rung Mr Phillips yet to tell him how she's doing?" Ty asked Amy, as they stopped to let Melody graze for a few moments.

Amy shook her head, remembering that she had been going to. "I will. I was going to last night but then," she hesitated. "Well … something happened."

She saw Ty's curious look and knew that she couldn't keep it from him any longer. When she had finished relating the events of the previous evening, his reaction was much the same as Soraya's – concerned, understanding.

"It must have been a real shock for you," he said, frowning.

"It was," Amy admitted. "But I'm not going to see him." She spoke the words more confidently than she had on the bus. The more she said them, the more she felt herself believing in them.

Ty nodded. "I can understand why."

"Lou doesn't," Amy said quietly.

Ty looked at her sympathetically. "It'll be OK," he said. "You'll see."

Amy wished she could believe him. Just the thought of Daddy coming back caused a wave of panic to well up inside her. She looked quickly at Melody and changed the subject. "Here, you hold her," she said, handing Ty the lead-rope. "She's hardly looking at you at all now."

Ty took the lead-rope and moved closer. Melody sidestepped away from him. "Easy, girl," he murmured.

Melody glanced at him suspiciously for a moment but then, to Amy's relief, she relaxed and began to crop at the short winter grass again. Ty reached out and gently stroked the mare's neck. She didn't flinch or move away.

"She's beginning to accept you," Amy said softly.

Ty nodded. "We'll get there in the end," he replied. "We'll just have to be patient and take things slowly for a while."

They had just put Melody back in her stall when Ben came into the barn. "Hi, there," he said, seeing Amy. "So, has Ty been telling you about our mystery visitor?"

"Mystery visitor?" Amy echoed.

"Oh, it was just this guy who came up to the house," Ty said dismissively. "Your grandpa said he was looking for casual work."

"He stayed for quite a while, you know," Ben said. "And before he went he kept looking at the stalls." He tapped his nose. "You know, I think he was a journalist in disguise."

"Yeah, right." Amy couldn't help smiling. "Like all those millions of other journalists who are beating down our door to get a story."

"You never know," Ben said.

Ty grinned at Amy. "He hasn't stopped going on about this all day. *Journalist*! He was just some guy looking for work. I guess word is getting around that we're doing well up here." He shut Melody's door. "Ivy, Solo and Sundance need riding. We could take them out on the trails."

Amy ran down to the house to get her hard hat. Grandpa and Lou were in the kitchen.

"Hi," Amy said, grabbing her hat from the easy chair by the TV.

Lou didn't say anything, she just carried on looking through the yard diary, but Grandpa smiled and looked up from the seed catalogue he was reading. "Hi, honey."

"I'm just going out for a ride with Ty and Ben," Amy said. As she reached the door, she remembered the conversation in the barn. "Oh, who was that man who called round today, Grandpa?"

To her surprise, Grandpa started violently in his chair.

"A man?" Lou said, looking up curiously.

The shocked expression on Jack Bartlett's face quickly smoothed out. "It was just someone looking for casual work," he said, his voice light. "You were out, Lou. It was no big deal."

"Ben seems to think it was." Amy grinned. "He's

convinced he was an undercover reporter. Or maybe it was a spy sent by Green Briar," she offered, with a laugh. Green Briar was a rival stable across town.

Lou shook her head and turned back to the diary. But when Amy glanced at Grandpa, his face looked taut with distress. "Are you OK, Grandpa?" she asked in concern.

"Me?" Jack said in surprise.

"Yeah, you don't look like yourself," Amy said.

Jack looked down at his hands. "Oh, I'm just a little tired. Old age catching up with me, that's all. I'm fine." He smiled at her but she noticed that his eyes looked distracted. "Just fine."

Amy smiled back, but she couldn't help feeling slightly concerned. Grandpa was very fit and healthy and, although he was sixty-eight years old now, he hardly ever showed any signs of old age. Hoping that he was telling the truth, Amy went back outside.

Over the next few days, Amy continued to notice that Grandpa didn't seem to be his usual self. Quieter than normal, he appeared to be lost in thought. Amy was consumed with thought as well – wondering what the day's mail would bring. But by Friday there was still no reply to Lou's letter.

Amy sighed as she groomed Melody on Friday night. "What's going to happen?" she wondered out loud.

Melody pulled at a pile of hay on the floor, her teeth chomping comfortably on the sweet-smelling stalks. Amy patted her. Looking after Melody helped her stop thinking about her father. With good food and daily grooming sessions, the mare's chestnut coat was at last beginning to shine dark and conker-like and her skin had lost its dryness. The hollows in her flanks had begun to fill out and – most importantly of all to Amy – the wariness had left her eyes. Through careful, patient attention, Melody was beginning to allow both Ty and Ben to handle her. But although she tolerated them, she didn't whicker to them or watch out for them like she did with Amy.

Amy stroked the mare's smooth neck. "You're going to have the most beautiful foal," she said, watching Melody's side twitch with a sudden kick. "And it'll go out in the fields with you and graze on the grass and gallop at your side. Won't that be wonderful?"

There was a noise at the stall door and Amy swung round. Ty was standing there, car keys in hand. "One day I'm going to put a tape-recorder in here," he said with a grin. "It would make very interesting listening."

"You talk to the horses too," Amy protested.

"I don't have complete conversations with them," Ty teased. He shook his head. "Well, I'm off home. I'll see you tomorrow. I was thinking of going to the cemetery to visit your mom's grave at lunch-time. Do you want to come?"

"I'd like that," Amy said. She tried to go to the cemetery as often as possible but with the darker evenings and the winter chores it was getting more difficult to find time to visit.

"I'll get some flowers," Ty said.

Amy nodded. "See you tomorrow, then."

"Yeah, later," Ty said and he left.

The next day, at lunch-time, Amy and Ty got into his battered pick-up and set off for the cemetery.

"I haven't been over there for a few weeks," Ty said.

"Me neither," Amy replied. "We've been so busy. I was going to go last weekend but then Melody arrived." She paused. "I wonder what Mom would have done with Melody?" She often found herself wondering how her mom would have treated the new horses that came to them. She knew that she had to rely on her own intuition and knowledge, but it was hard not to wonder whether Mom would have done things differently.

Ty looked at her reassuringly. "Probably exactly the same as you. Melody's wound's healing well, she's putting on condition and getting over her nervousness. You're doing a great job."

"I guess," Amy said, feeling a bit happier. "I just hope that the birth goes without a hitch. Now that we know the foal's alive, I hope it's healthy."

Ty nodded and they drove on in silence.

Finally they reached the parking lot and got out. Tall trees loomed overhead, their bare branches outlined against the dull grey sky. It was a cold, frosty day and as they walked down the path towards Marion's grave, their breath froze like white smoke in the air.

"I wonder when we'll get the first snow," Ty said, as their boots crunched on the freshly gritted stone path.

Amy nodded. When it snowed, the workload at Heartland increased – the water troughs froze, the yard became icy and the ground in the schooling rings became hard so there was less chance to exercise the horses. She dug her hands in her pockets and hoped that the snow would hold off for a while longer.

They rounded the corner that led to the quiet area of the cemetery where Marion was buried. Suddenly Amy stopped. "Hey, look!" she exclaimed.

A man was kneeling by her mom's grave, his head bowed. Hearing her voice, he looked round and rose swiftly to his feet. He was tall with slightly greying hair. He looked like he'd once been handsome but now deep lines were etched across his face.

A swift rush of anger rose inside Amy. What was this stranger doing? "Who are you?" she demanded hotly. She began to run down the path towards him. "What are you doing? This is my mom's grave."

The man stared at her and, for a moment, she thought he was going to speak. His mouth opened, but then a strange hunted look crossed his face and he suddenly turned and moved off across the grass.

Amy stopped and stared after the figure – noticing as he hurried away that he had a limp. She swung round to Ty. "Did you see that?" she demanded indignantly.

Ty was frowning.

"What is it?" Amy said.

"It was the man who came over to the farm the other day looking for work," Ty replied. "I'm sure of it."

Amy stared at him. "What was he doing here?"

"I don't know," Ty said, sounding mystified. "Maybe he *is* a reporter," he added, trying to break the tension.

Amy looked after the figure, but he had vanished into the mist.

"He was kneeling beside Mom's grave!" Amy told Grandpa and Lou indignantly when she arrived back at Heartland half an hour later. "I went over to speak to him but he just ran away."

The two of them had been eating lunch and now Lou put down her knife and fork. "And Ty said it was the same person who came here the other day?"

"Yes! He was sure of it," Amy said hotly. Now her initial shock had passed, she felt angry. Who was this person and what had he been doing at her mom's grave? It was creepy and weird.

Lou frowned and turned to Grandpa. "Did this guy say anything about knowing Mom when he came round?"

For a moment, Jack looked as if he was about to shake his

head but then he seemed to stop himself and, for the first time, Amy noticed that the muscles in his face were tense. A red tinge spread along his cheekbones.

"Grandpa, what is it?" Amy said, seeing his guarded expression.

Grandpa didn't speak.

Amy's heart suddenly began to thump in her chest. There was something wrong – something dreadfully wrong.

"Grandpa?" Lou said, and from the high tone of her voice Amy could tell that Grandpa's expression was unnerving her too.

Jack cleared his throat. "There's ... something you should know," he said. He looked at Amy. "The man you saw – the man who came round the other day – isn't just a stranger. He's..." He took a deep breath. "He's your father."

Chapter Six

For a moment the world stood still, and then the room and everything in it seemed to rush away from Amy at high speed. She clutched the back of the chair she was standing behind. "What?" she stammered in shock.

"That man is your father," Grandpa repeated.

"It isn't true!" Amy cried.

"No!" Lou gasped, almost at the same time.

Amy's gaze frantically scanned her grandpa's face, desperately looking for him to shake his head, to smile. But he didn't. His blue eyes were grave. "I should have told you right from the start," he said heavily. "It was wrong of me. When he came over, I told him that you didn't want to see him. I told him to leave."

"You did *what*?" Lou burst out, pushing her chair back violently.

Amy jumped – through shock of the announcement she had almost forgotten about Lou. Now she saw that furious colour was flooding her sister's cheeks.

"You told Daddy to go away?" Lou said, staring at Grandpa. "How *could* you?" she cried, her voice rising. "You know how much I want to see him!"

"Yes, I know," Jack said, sounding wretched. "But, Lou, I had to." He stood up and stepped towards her. "I was the one who had to pick up the pieces after he left your mother. I saw how he almost destroyed her, Lou. I couldn't have him here."

He reached out for her, but Lou jerked her arm away. "Don't touch me!" She stared at him. "I'll never forgive you for this, Grandpa!" she spat, her eyes welling with tears. "Never!"

"Lou…" Amy said, going towards her

"No! Leave me alone!" Lou cried. With a sob, she grabbed her car keys off the side and then ran out of the kitchen, slamming the back door.

"Lou!" Jack called. But by the time he and Amy had reached the doorway, Lou was already starting the engine of her car.

"What have I done?" Jack whispered, as Lou drove off at high speed. He turned, his face pale. "Oh, Amy, what have I done?"

Amy saw the despair in his eyes. "She'll be OK, Grandpa," she said, desperately trying to ignore the frantic hammering of her heart. "She'll come back soon."

* * *

But by six o'clock that evening Lou still hadn't come back. Amy had briefly explained to Ty what had happened, and after the horses had been fed he had come down to the house to wait with her and Grandpa.

"It's been three hours now," Grandpa said, getting up and pacing across the floor. "Where is she?"

"Maybe she's gone to Scott's?" Ty suggested.

Grandpa picked up the phone and began to dial the vet's number.

Ty pressed Amy's hand. "You OK?" he asked.

Amy nodded numbly. Since her grandpa had made the announcement, her mind had gone into shock. Every so often an image of the man – her father – standing by the grave flashed into her mind, but each time she pushed it away. To think that she had actually seen Daddy, spoken to him and not recognized him, was just too much to deal with. To stop herself thinking about it she focused her mind on Lou. Where had she gone? Was she all right?

She looked at Ty and saw the concern in his green eyes. "Lou will be fine," he murmured, squeezing her hand again. "She just needs some time to cool off."

Amy swallowed and looked down. She desperately wanted to believe him but she couldn't help thinking the worst. What if Lou had been involved in an accident? It was almost dark outside and it had begun to rain – the roads would be wet and slippery. She fought back the fear that rose inside her as memories flashed into her mind, memories of a day five months ago when she and Mom had been driving through the rain. In her mind, she saw the sodden road, the sleeting rain, the trailer skidding towards the fallen tree...

"Scott — it's Jack here."

The sound of her grandpa's voice jerked Amy from her nightmare thoughts. Her eyes scanned his face as he asked if Scott had seen Lou. There was a pause and then Amy saw the hope die from his eyes and knew what the answer had been.

"She left here over three hours ago," she heard Grandpa say. "We had an argument. It's too difficult to explain over the phone but she's upset — very upset."

He replaced the handset. "Scott's coming round."

Just then, the back door opened and Ben came in. "I'm off home now, if that's OK," he said, stamping his feet on the mat. He looked round at their worried faces. "Is everything all right?"

Amy nodded. She had simply told him that there had been a family disagreement. "Yeah, you call it a day," she said, forcing herself to smile. "We'll be fine."

"You're sure there isn't anything I can do?" Ben asked.

Amy shook her head. "See you tomorrow."

"Bye, then," Ben said.

Amy and Ty sat in silence while Grandpa paced up and down.

After twenty minutes, Scott arrived. He came into the kitchen, shaking the raindrops off his jacket.

"So what exactly happened?" he asked quickly.

As Jack explained, the concern on Scott's face deepened. "And she just took off without saying where she was going?"

Grandpa nodded. "I tried to stop her, but she wouldn't listen." He stood by the sink and rubbed his face with his hands. "I should never have done what I did," he said to Scott, with a sigh, "but when Tim just turned up, I couldn't stop myself. I know how he almost destroyed Marion and I couldn't stand by and see him upset my granddaughters." He looked wretchedly at Amy. "Please try and understand, honey, I was just trying to protect you – to protect us all."

Amy hated seeing the guilt on his face. "I know, Grandpa," she said, going over and hugging him. "And I do understand. But I ... I don't know if Lou will." She swallowed, her eyes catching Ty's.

"You said you saw your father at the cemetery?" Scott asked her.

Amy nodded.

"Maybe Lou went there," he said abruptly. "She might have thought that he would go back." He took his car keys out of his pocket. "I'll go and take a look."

"I'll come too," Amy offered. At least then she would be doing something, not just waiting around.

"Sure thing," Scott said. He turned to Jack. "Call us if she arrives back. I've got my phone – and we'll let you know if we find her."

* * *

Scott's jeep bumped down the driveway. Rain spattered on to the windscreen and the wipers beat methodically as they swung back and forth. Amy huddled deeper into her coat. *Please, please let us find Lou*, she prayed.

She glanced at Scott's face. The skin around his mouth and chin were taut with worry. "What was Jack thinking of?" he muttered savagely, as they turned on to the road.

"He was just trying to do what he thought was best," Amy said hotly, jumping immediately to her grandpa's defence. "He didn't want us to get hurt."

"But he *knows* how Lou feels about your father," Scott said.

Amy didn't answer. She could see why Scott was siding with Lou but she also fully understood her grandpa's actions. It must have been awful for him to have watched Mom suffering after Daddy had left. And equally, it must have been impossibly difficult for him to meet Daddy again.

Daddy. The word rang in Amy's ears. She had seen her father – even spoken to him. An image of his face sprang into her mind. The deeply etched lines, the hunted look in his eyes. She shut her eyes, willing it to go away.

Neither she nor Scott spoke again until they reached the cemetery. There were no lights on and the wrought-iron gates that led into the memorial ground were shut and locked. The mist from earlier had grown thicker and now it swirled about the deserted car park. Suddenly, Amy caught sight of a single, lonely car parked under the leafless canopy of an oak tree.

"That's Lou's Honda!" she gasped.

Scott put his foot on the accelerator and his jeep shot across the car park, stopping with a screech of brakes behind Lou's car. Even before the jeep had completely stopped, Amy was leaping out. She ran to the driver's door, her heart pounding.

The windows were frosted over but Amy could just make out a shadowy figure sitting huddled in the front seat.

"Lou!" she cried out, banging on the window.

The next moment, Amy saw her sister's face looking round at her.

Amy tried the door, but it was locked. "Open the door, Lou!"

For a moment Lou didn't move, but then, with fumbling fingers, she released the catch.

Amy flung the door open. "We've been so worried!"

Lou stared at her, her face white. "He wasn't here. I waited and waited and he didn't come back." Suddenly her face crumpled and a strangled sob burst from her. "Oh, Amy, now I'm never going to see him again!"

Amy flung her arms round her sister's neck. "You will," she gabbled. "He'll get back in touch and, if he doesn't, we'll find him, Lou. I'll help you."

"Do you mean that?" Lou sobbed.

"Yes!" Amy felt prepared to say anything to comfort her sister. She was so relieved that Lou was safe.

They hugged tightly.

"Lou! Are you all right?" Scott's deep voice spoke from behind Amy.

"Scott," Lou said, pulling back from Amy in confusion and looking up at him. "What are you doing here?"

"Jack told me what happened," Scott said quickly. "Are you OK?"

Lou nodded.

Scott crouched down and spoke softly. "I've been so worried." He took her hands. "You're freezing." He tightened his grip on her fingers. "Come on, let's get you home. We'll pick up your car tomorrow."

Lou looked too worn out to argue. She got out of the car without a word and allowed Scott to put his jacket over her shoulders. Wrapping an arm around her waist, he helped her into the jeep.

The back seat was crowded with boxes of medicines, plastic gloves, waterproofs and map books. Amy pushed them to one side and climbed in. The first wild rush of relief she had felt when they found that Lou was OK was fading, and she was beginning to feel anxious about what would happen when they got back home.

As soon as the jeep drew up outside the house, the back door opened and Grandpa and Ty ran out. Amy had phoned them on Scott's mobile phone to let them know that Lou was safe.

"Lou!" Grandpa exclaimed, hurrying over as Lou got out of the jeep. "Thank heavens you're all right."

Lou ignored him and marched into the house without saying a word. With a look at her grandpa's hurt face, Amy ran after Lou.

"Lou!" she said, catching up with her sister in the kitchen. "Grandpa's been really worried about you."

Lou swung round and Amy braced herself for a furious retort, but then Lou checked herself. When she spoke, her voice was quiet. "I'm not ready to talk to him right now, Amy," she said, the hurt showing in her eyes. "I just can't."

Scott, Grandpa and Ty appeared in the doorway.

"I'm going to my room," Lou said bleakly.

"Lou," Grandpa said quickly. "We need to talk this through."

"There's nothing to discuss," Lou answered curtly. She glanced at Scott. "Thanks for coming to find me," she said wearily. "I'll … I'll ring you tomorrow."

Scott smiled. "Take care." He looked like he wanted to say more, but the presence of the others seemed to hold him back. "Get some rest," he said.

Lou nodded and then turned and walked out of the room. There was a silence.

"I'd better go," Scott said at last. He glanced at Amy. "Bye."

Amy felt tears rise in her eyes as he left. Everything was going wrong.

Ty put a hand on her shoulder. "Maybe it's best if I go too," he said, looking at her and Jack. "You've got family things to sort out." He hugged Amy briefly. "I'll see you tomorrow."

Grandpa made an effort to smile. "Thanks for staying, Ty."

"No problem," Ty said. "I'm just glad nothing happened to Lou." With a last look at Amy, he left.

Grandpa sat down at the table. "Oh, Amy," he groaned, putting his head in his hands. "What am I going to do?"

Amy sat down beside him, wishing she could say something to comfort him. "It'll be OK," she managed. "Lou will come round in the end."

Grandpa looked up at her. "What about you? How do *you* feel? Do you want to meet your father?"

A vivid image of the man she had seen that afternoon at her mom's grave flashed into Amy's mind. She swallowed. "I didn't recognize him, Grandpa," she whispered, voicing the thought that had been haunting her all afternoon. "I didn't know who he was."

"But how could you?" Jack replied. "You haven't seen him for twelve years, and you were only a toddler when he left."

Amy looked down. Maybe Grandpa was right, but it didn't make her feel any better. How could she have not known Daddy? How could she not have felt even the faintest glimmer of recognition?

Jack took her hand. "Amy, you mustn't blame yourself for not knowing him. It's his fault for not being around when you were growing up."

Amy lifted worried eyes to his. "But..."

"There are no buts," Grandpa said firmly. He put his arms

around her and hugged her tightly. "Your father chose to leave and not to stay in touch."

Amy felt the rough wool of his pullover tickle her cheek. "He did write to Mom that time," she said.

"Yes," Grandpa said quietly. "He did."

Amy glanced up at him. "Did ... did she ever talk to you about that, Grandpa?" Until she and Lou had found the letter she hadn't had any idea that Daddy had ever written. How had Mom felt?

"She showed it to me the day it arrived," Grandpa said. The wrinkles on his face seeming to deepen as he remembered. "I ... I felt like killing him."

He must have seen Amy's shocked look because he shook his head. "So many years had passed. Your mom had built a new life for herself, she was just starting to find happiness and then he wrote and almost destroyed everything again. Just the sight of his handwriting was enough to make her seriously consider giving up everything she had here and going back to him. She loved him, Amy. Despite everything he had done, she loved him to the end."

"But she didn't go back," Amy said wonderingly. "Why?"

"I think, ultimately, she realized that whatever she and your father had once had between them had been irreversibly spoilt, and that going back could never be the same," Grandpa replied. "After she showed me the letter, we didn't really discuss it any further. We both knew it was a decision she had to make on her own." He kissed the top of

Amy's head. "She made the right decision, Amy. For herself – and for the family."

Amy rested her head silently against him and thought about her mom. It must have been a dreadfully hard decision to make, particularly if she had still loved Daddy. And poor Grandpa. How he must have suffered, seeing what his daughter had gone through. Amy didn't blame him for hating their father – or for turning him away. But would Lou ever understand that?

Chapter Seven

The next morning when Amy got up and went downstairs to feed the horses, she found Grandpa already in the kitchen getting out the breakfast things. His eyes looked tired. "How did you sleep?" he asked.

Amy had slept restlessly, her dreams full of images of her daddy standing by her mother's grave. "Badly," she admitted, going over to the fridge.

"That makes two of us," Grandpa said.

Just then, the door opened and Lou came in. The air in the kitchen suddenly seemed to stiffen.

"Hi, Lou," Amy said, trying to act normal. "Do you want some orange juice?"

Lou shook her head. "No thanks." She sat down at the table. She was dressed but looked tired and pale.

Grandpa put down the plates he had in his hand. "Did you sleep?" he asked her.

Lou shrugged. "On and off."

For a moment, Grandpa looked as if he was about to turn away but then he changed his mind and sat down. "Look, Lou," he said. "I know what I did was wrong, but we can't let it come between us."

Amy watched her sister look at him with something resembling hope in her eyes.

"I've reached a decision," Grandpa continued. "Although I won't have your father here at Heartland, I can't – and I won't – stand in your way if you still want to find him."

Lou looked at him incredulously. "Did you really think you'd have been able to *stop* me?" she said, her voice rising.

"Lou..." Amy began, but her sister didn't even look at her. She had got to her feet and was staring at Grandpa.

"This is Daddy we're talking about, Grandpa," she said angrily. "He's my father and I love him."

"I know you do, Lou," Jack Bartlett replied. "I'm just saying that I don't want him here at Heartland."

Lou shook her head and walked to the door. "I'm going to Scott's."

"You can't, Lou," Amy said, hurrying after her as she went outside. "Your car isn't here."

Lou paused for barely a second. "Then I'll walk," she said.

Grandpa joined Amy. "Don't be crazy, Lou. It's miles!"

For a fraction of a second, Amy thought that Lou was going to snap back but she didn't, she just took a deep breath. "A walk will do me good," she said, her voice level. "I need some space."

Grandpa sighed. "Look, if you really want to go, Lou, I'll give you a lift. You can't walk all that way."

Lou hesitated, but just then both Ty and Ben's cars came up the drive. A look of relief crossed her face. "It's OK," she said. "Ty will take me."

Lou ran over to Ty's pick-up and opened the passenger door, then climbed in. The truck turned around and headed down the driveway.

Amy glanced at Grandpa. With a muttered exclamation he strode back into the house.

Ben, meanwhile, had parked and strolled over. "What's going on?" he asked.

"Nothing," Amy snapped unhappily.

She saw a hurt look cross Ben's face. Turning quickly, he marched up to the feed-room. Amy kicked a nearby stone in frustration. Right now, she just didn't feel like coping with one of Ben's moods. Frowning, she went up the yard after him.

Ben was banging the buckets down on to the stone floor. Ignoring him, Amy began to scoop grain into them. Neither of them spoke a word.

Eventually, Amy could stand the atmosphere no longer. "I'll take these to the back barn," she said abruptly, picking up a pile of feed buckets. "You finish off here."

Ben didn't reply. Glad to escape, Amy carried the feed buckets up the yard.

The horses in the barn were all looking over their doors. Seeing Amy, they whinnied excitedly.

"OK, OK, I'm here," Amy called, starting to empty the feeds into the mangers. She reached Melody's stall last. The chestnut mare nickered softly as Amy came to her door.

"Hi, girl," Amy said, letting herself into the stall.

Melody nuzzled her shoulder as Amy tipped her feed into the manger. Amy let out a long sigh and watched the mare thrust her nose eagerly into the grain and begin to eat.

She put her arm round Melody's neck, taking comfort from the mare's warm, solid presence. Everything was so confused. Grandpa and Lou had never argued like this before. And what about Daddy? Amy turned her face into the mare's rough mane.

"I didn't recognize him, Melody," she whispered despairingly. "I didn't know who he was."

She felt warm breath on the back of her neck and looked round. As if sensing her unhappiness, Melody had turned her head to look at her. Lifting her nose, she gently nuzzled Amy's hair.

Amy swallowed. It was something her mom's horse, Pegasus, used to do before he'd died. Tears filled her eyes. "Oh, Melody," she whispered in despair. "I don't know what to do."

Ty arrived back just after Amy and Ben had finished feeding and watering the horses. "So, what's been going on?" he said curiously to Amy. "Lou hardly said a word on the way over to Scott's."

"She had an argument with Grandpa this morning," Amy replied, trying to sound composed. "And last night."

"Any sign of them sorting it out?" Ty asked.

Amy shook her head.

"How are you feeling?" Ty asked, looking at her in concern.

Before Amy could answer, the phone rang. "I'll get it," she said, knowing that Grandpa would probably be getting dressed.

She ran down the yard and into the kitchen. "Heartland," she said. "Amy Fleming here."

"Hi, this is Judy Stillman. I was wondering if I might speak to Ben."

"I'll just get him," Amy said. Seeing a wheelbarrow by Red's stall, she went over. "Your mom's on the phone," she called.

"I'm not speaking to her," Ben replied tersely. "Tell her I'm busy."

"Go and tell her yourself," Amy retorted angrily.

Ben glared at her. "I don't want to talk to her!"

It was the last straw. Amy's temper finally snapped. "Oh, come on, Ben!" she exploded. "Stop behaving like a five-year-old! Just go and speak to her."

"No!" Ben said furiously.

"Well, I'm not going to!" Amy yelled. "You can't put me in the middle of it."

Ty came hurrying over. "What's going on?" he demanded.

"He won't go and speak to his mom," Amy said, turning to Ty for support. "She's on the phone."

"Ben, stop being so dumb," Ty said curtly. "Go and take the call."

Ben looked as if he were about to argue for a moment but then he turned and stormed down the yard to the house.

Amy watched him, but Ty just shook his head and went back to the chores.

Amy waited at the top of the stable block for Ben to finish with the call. She felt she had to apologize for overreacting. But when Ben came back, he just grabbed his pitchfork and headed towards Red's stall, clearly ignoring Amy.

"Ben!" Amy exclaimed, going after him.

He swung round furiously. "Look, I spoke to her, didn't I? Now just leave me alone. I've got to get back to the mucking out."

Amy was almost out of her mind with exasperation. "The mucking out! As if *that*'s important!"

Ben stiffened. "Oh, sorry, I forgot," he spat. "Nothing I do here is important, is it?"

"What are you talking about?" Amy demanded.

"Nothing I do matters," Ben shouted. "You and Ty treat the horses, I'm just a stable-hand. It makes no difference how hard I work – anyone could do what I do. Basically, there's all of the rest of you – and then there's me."

Amy was completely taken aback. "But that's crazy," she said in astonishment. "We don't think like that."

"No?" Ben said disbelievingly. "So how come you never tell me what's going on?" Turning on his heel, he marched back to Red's stall.

Amy was stunned. She'd had no idea Ben felt so left out. She paused for a moment and then went after him. She had to sort this out.

He was angrily forking straw into the wheelbarrow.

"Ben," Amy said but he didn't look up or even acknowledge her presence. "Look, I'm sorry," she said quickly. "I wasn't leaving you out on purpose. I just wasn't ready to talk about what's going on. It's kind of complicated."

Ben seemed to hesitate for a moment, but still he didn't look up.

Amy swallowed. "It's my dad," she said to his back. "You know he left us twelve years ago? Well, Lou's been in touch with him recently and he tried to visit the other day. He was the man that Grandpa said was looking for casual work."

Ben turned quickly. "That guy?"

Amy nodded and quickly explained everything else that had happened. "So now Lou's mad with Grandpa and Grandpa's determined not to have him come here," she concluded. She looked at his astonished face. "I ... I told you it was complicated."

Ben nodded. "Yeah, I see." The fire had faded completely

from his eyes and he looked awkward. "Thanks for telling me."

"I should have told you before," Amy said. "You're part of Heartland now."

Ben looked away. "Yeah, whatever," he muttered, not sounding as if he believed her.

"You *are*," Amy insisted.

Ben turned back to the straw bed. After watching him for a few moments longer, Amy shook her head and walked away.

She found Ty in the back barn. "Still in one piece?" he said with a grin. "Who came off worst – you or Ben?"

Amy was in no mood to be teased. She told him quickly about what Ben had said. "He doesn't feel he's important here," she said.

"But that's stupid," Ty said.

"It's what he thinks," Amy replied. "I explained to him what's going on with Lou and Grandpa but it didn't seem to make much of a difference."

Ty frowned. "We need to talk to him."

"I tried," said Amy, "but he wouldn't listen."

"Try again later," Ty said. "Say you need to see Gypsy being ridden by someone else or something like that and go out for a ride with him. It might be easier to get him to talk about it away from here."

Amy nodded. "OK, but what about you? Will you come?"

Ty shook his head. "He'll probably open up more if it's

just the two of you. If it doesn't work out, then we'll speak to him together."

Two hours later, Amy and Ben rode out of Heartland on Moochie and Gypsy. The wind had got up and the horses jogged excitedly. Amy patted Moochie's bay neck. "Let's go on the Field Trail," she said. "It'll be more sheltered than up on the mountain."

Ben nodded and they turned on to the trail that led down into the valley. They rode along the grassy path in silence. Amy tried to think of a way to begin the conversation she wanted to have, but whenever she glanced at Ben the sight of his set profile made the words die on her tongue. What could she say? However she started, it was going to be a very awkward conversation.

Moochie pulled at his reins and Amy chickened out. "Shall we trot?" she said, telling herself it could wait a bit.

"OK," Ben said shortly.

Amy clicked her tongue and Moochie leapt eagerly into a trot. The trees on either side of the trail were swaying in the wind and Moochie's mane blew over Amy's hands. She looked across at Gypsy. The black mare was throwing up her head, looking as if she wanted to go faster, but Ben controlled her effortlessly.

"Gypsy's going well for you," Amy called.

They trotted round a bend in the track. Suddenly both Moochie and Gypsy shied violently. A pile of plastic barrels covered with sheets of tarpaulin had been left standing at the side of the trail. The tarpaulin flapped wildly in the wind.

Quickly recovering her balance, Amy brought Moochie under control and glanced round at Ben. He was soothing Gypsy, who was backing off from the barrels, trembling.

"It's OK, girl," Amy heard him saying. "They won't hurt."

"I'll go first," Amy called, hoping that if Gypsy saw Moochie walk past the barrels then she would follow. She closed her legs on Moochie's sides. "Walk on," she said. But just as the big bay stepped forward, the tarpaulin flapped furiously and Moochie shied back again.

"Here, I'll have a go," Ben said. He shortened his reins and urged Gypsy on. The black mare snorted, her eyes wide. But Ben insisted. Lifting her feet high, Gypsy approached the barrels, every muscle in her body tense.

Just then a huge gust of wind blew under the tarpaulin and tore it free from its remaining rope. It twirled upwards. With a frightened whinny, Gypsy plunged sideways but the wind tossed the tarpaulin towards her and the next moment it had caught behind her saddle.

With a terrified snort, Gypsy began to buck viciously.

"Ben!" Amy gasped in horror. But then Moochie, frightened by the noise of the tarpaulin and Gypsy's bucking, wheeled round on his haunches and galloped in the opposite direction.

Within a few strides, Amy managed to pull him up and swing him round. Gypsy's bucking had loosened the sheet of tarpaulin from behind her saddle and it was now twirling away across the field. But Gypsy seemed oblivious. With her head between her knees, she was bucking wildly.

Amy's stomach somersaulted. There was no way Ben could stay on. She waited for him to come crashing to the ground. But he didn't, his body moved with the horse, his strong legs and seat anchoring him in the saddle. After three more bucks, he managed to pull Gypsy's head up. Amy saw his lips moving constantly as he sought to quiet the frightened mare. At long last, she came to a trembling halt.

"Are you OK, Ben?" Amy exclaimed, kicking Moochie and trotting forward.

Ben was leaning low over Gypsy's neck, his hands stroking and soothing as he calmed her down. He looked round.

"That was exciting," he said with a grin.

Amy stared at him in amazement. After what he had just been through, how could he smile like that? "How did you stay on?" she stammered.

"I guess it's just this special glue that I use," Ben joked.

"If you'd fallen off we'd have been back to square one," Amy said, suddenly realizing how lucky they'd been that Ben had stayed on and that all their work with Gypsy hadn't been ruined. "You were fantastic!"

Ben looked embarrassed. "It's no big deal," he said awkwardly.

"It is!" Amy exclaimed, riding Moochie up to Gypsy. "You were brilliant!"

But Ben didn't look convinced. "Anyone could have stayed on."

"They couldn't," Amy said. "Ben! You're an amazing rider." She saw the doubt on his face and all the words that she had been wanting to say tumbled out of her. "Stop putting yourself down all the time. You're crazy to think that we don't need you at Heartland. We do – we really do!"

Ben hesitated for a moment. "Do you mean that?"

"Yes!" Amy cried. "Heartland just wouldn't be the same without you."

A pleased flush of colour crossed Ben's face. "Thanks," he said. "That really means a lot, Amy."

"It's the truth," she said simply. She grinned at him. "You're part of Heartland now – whether you like it or not."

To her relief, Ben smiled back. "I like it," he said.

They exchanged smiles and then Ben picked up his reins and asked Gypsy to walk on. "Looks like you were right about her," he said, changing the subject quickly. "She's not ready to go home yet."

"Definitely not," Amy agreed as she rode along the trail beside him. "So, are you looking forward to the show?" she asked, happy to go along with the change of subject now that the tension between them had subsided.

Ben nodded. "Yeah, I am. You and Soraya are still going to come, aren't you?"

"Of course," Amy said.

They rode on for a few more minutes in silence and then

Ben spoke. "You ... you know when my mom rang this morning," he said.

Amy nodded. How could she forget!

"Well, she can make it to the show after all," Ben said. "She's changed her meeting."

"But that's great!" Amy exclaimed. She saw the frown on his face. "Isn't it?" she asked uncertainly.

Ben looked down at Gypsy's neck. "I don't care what she does," he said. "She doesn't care about me."

Amy stared at him. "But she's your mom."

"So?" Ben said. He shook his head bitterly. "I've never meant anything to her."

"I don't believe that's true," Amy said, thinking about the hurt in Mrs Stillman's voice the day Ben had refused to speak to her on the phone.

"No?" Ben said. "Then why did she send me to live with my aunt? She just wanted me out of the way."

"I thought it was because you were getting into trouble," Amy said, remembering what she had been told about Ben's past. "You were skipping school, weren't you?" She stared at his face. "If she hadn't cared then she wouldn't have done anything, Ben. It can't have been easy for her."

"Well, it wasn't easy for me either!" Ben exclaimed furiously. He shook his head. "What do you understand about it anyway? Your mom never abandoned you!" Almost before the words were out he seemed to regret them. He paled but Amy hardly noticed. She was too angry.

"No! But my dad did!" she cried, incensed. "*My* mom's dead." Hot tears sprang to her eyes. "You don't know how lucky you are, Ben," she yelled. "I can't believe you won't give her another chance."

Desperate to hide her tears, Amy dug her heels into Moochie's side. With a surprised snort, he leapt forward into a canter. Amy urged him on. She heard Ben yell at her to stop, but she ignored him. She wanted to get away from him – away from everything.

"Faster!" she sobbed to Moochie. "Faster!"

Moochie's canter became a gallop, his hooves pounding across the damp grass. The wind buffeted against Amy's face, whipping tears from her eyes. She dug her heels in, running away from Ben – running away from her thoughts.

Through the mist of tears, she saw that they were approaching the sharp right-angled bend at the end of the track. She knew that they would never make it at such high speed but, for one wild moment, she didn't care. Ben, Lou, Grandpa, Daddy – the only way to forget them was to keep on going faster.

Suddenly she heard the sound of hooves behind her. She glanced over her shoulder. Urged on by Ben, Gypsy was catching up. Ben leant low over the black mare's neck. "Stop, Amy!" he yelled. "You'll never make the corner!"

Ignoring him, Amy urged Moochie on towards the bend, but in three powerful strides, Gypsy had drawn level. Leaning over her neck, Ben grabbed at Moochie's reins.

Feeling Ben's hands grasping the leather, Moochie jerked his head up, his haunches skidding underneath him. Amy was flung back in the saddle and it was only by grasping a handful of Moochie's mane that she stopped herself from falling off.

"What are you doing?" she screamed at Ben.

"Me!" he yelled back. "What about you? Have you gone mad?"

Amy was about to scream back when suddenly she saw the corner, only a metre ahead of them, and realized how close she had come to hurting Moochie. At that speed, crashing off the path would have been devastating. Amy's emotions, stretched taut by the events of the last few days, snapped, and a sob burst from her. Scrambling down from Moochie's back, she collapsed on the ground and buried her head in her hands.

Within a few seconds, Ben had dismounted and was kneeling beside her. "It's OK," he said, putting an arm round her shaking shoulders. "Amy, don't cry. I should never have said what I did."

"It's not you," Amy said, distraught. "It's everything – everything's all gone wrong."

"Things will sort themselves out," Ben said. "You'll see."

"How can they?" Amy cried. "Grandpa and Lou are never going to agree about Daddy. And what if he gets in touch again? What if Lou decides to leave Heartland and go and live with him?"

"It won't happen," Ben said, pulling her close and hugging her. But Amy knew they were empty words. Who could tell what was going to happen in the future? And who knew what would happen if Daddy did come back? Her tears fell faster.

Powerless to say anything to comfort her, Ben held her until, at long last, her sobs started to subside. Amy took a deep breath and looked up at him. "I'm sorry," she said, feeling horribly embarrassed. She rubbed her jacket sleeve across her face.

"Don't be," Ben said. "It's me that should be sorry. I shouldn't have piled my problems on to you like that."

"I don't mind," Amy said. She glanced at him and swallowed. There was something she had to say. "But you are lucky, Ben. You've still got your mom and it's not too late."

She saw Ben flinch and looked away. There was a long silence. Finally Amy gathered up the reins and put her foot in the stirrup. "Come on," she said, not looking at him. "We should go."

She mounted. When she looked round, she saw that Ben was still standing beside Gypsy.

"Ben?" she said. "Are you coming?"

He didn't answer her question. "You're right," he said quietly. "I guess I am lucky."

Not saying anything more, he mounted and clicked his tongue. The two horses moved forwards.

They rode in silence. Ben seemed lost in thought but Amy

hardly noticed. Her own thoughts were full of Lou and Grandpa and the situation at home.

As they approached Heartland again, Ben turned in his saddle. There was a decisive look on his face. "I'm going to ring my mom," he said.

The words jerked Amy out of her own thoughts and she stared at him. "You are?"

"Yes." Ben took a deep breath. "Whatever's happened, she's still my mom, and if she wants to come to the show then I'm not going to stop her."

Chapter Eight

Amy was untacking Moochie when Ty came to find her. "How did it go?" he asked her in a low voice.

After everything that had happened on the ride, Amy had almost forgotten that the reason for the ride had been to talk to Ben about his role at Heartland. "OK," she said. "I ... I think we sorted things out."

"Good," Ty said, looking relieved.

"I'll tell you about it later," Amy said, letting herself out of the stall.

As Amy headed for the tack-room, she heard Ben talking in Red's stall. She glanced in as she walked by, and saw him talking on his mobile phone. *All right*, Amy thought to herself, hoping the conversation with his mom was going well.

"So?" she demanded, hurrying over when he finally emerged. "How did it go?"

He shrugged. "Well, I told her she could come to the show."

"And she's going to?" Amy asked eagerly.

Ben nodded. "She's meeting me there." He ran a hand through his hair. "That's going to be fun – *not!*"

"It'll be fine," Amy said optimistically.

But Ben looked far from convinced.

Well, it may not have been a full-blown reconciliation, she thought as she walked away from Red's stall, *but at least Ben's speaking to his mom again – surely that's a step in the right direction.*

For the rest of the day, Ben was like a different person around the yard. He laughed and joked and even came down to the house to have lunch with Amy and Ty.

"Well, whatever you said to him seems to have worked," Ty said to Amy that afternoon, as they both filled water buckets at the trough. "I've never seen him so relaxed."

Amy had told Ty about Gypsy bucking and about her conversation with Ben afterwards, but she hadn't admitted to him about the way she had taken off on Moochie. It was something she felt ashamed of and wanted to forget.

"Best of all, he's got in touch with his mom," Amy said. "He's going to meet her at the show next week."

"Are you still planning to go and watch?" Ty asked.

"Yes," Amy said. "Why don't you come?"

"I'd like to," Ty replied. "But I've arranged to meet up with some friends that day – it's my day off."

Amy looked at him in surprise. Ty rarely went out unless it was to do something with horses. "Who are you meeting?" she asked.

"Pete and Greg — they're friends of mine from high school," Ty said. "It's been arranged for a while — a kind of reunion before they go off to college. I'd have liked to have made it to the show, though. I hope Ben does well. He's been working so hard with Red that he really deserves it."

Just then, the farmhouse door opened and Grandpa looked out. "Amy!" he called. "Phone call for you! It's Mr Phillips!"

Amy ran down to the kitchen and took the phone from her grandpa. "Hi," she said. "Amy speaking."

She heard the hesitancy in Mr Phillips's voice. "I ... I was just ringing to find out how Melody is," he said. "I hope you don't mind."

"Not at all," Amy said. She hadn't spoken to him since just after the accident. She had meant to ring him, but the events of the last few days had pushed all thoughts of calling him out of her mind. Now she was glad to be able to give him good news. "She's doing really well," Amy said. "Her wound's healing well and she's not showing any sign of going into labour." She remembered the best news of all. "And her foal's kicking strongly — so it must be alive."

"Oh, how wonderful," Ray Phillips gasped. Amy heard him take a deep, trembling breath. "I've been so worried," he admitted.

"Well, like I said, she's doing fine," Amy said.

"My wife would have been so pleased," Mr Phillips said quietly.

Amy heard the note of sadness in his voice. "Will you come and see the foal when it's born?" she asked.

"I'd love to," Ray Phillips replied. He paused. When he spoke again it was with difficulty. "Maybe, if I could just see it safe and sound, I'd feel that I hadn't done the wrong thing after all."

"I'll ring you and let you know as soon as the foal is born," Amy promised. "And, Mr Phillips," she added quickly, "I'm sure everything's going to turn out just fine."

When she put the phone down, she was thinking hard. Mr Phillips obviously still blamed himself for Melody's accident. She hoped that if he did come and see the mare and her foal, both alive and well, that he really would stop giving himself such a tough time over his decision. Amy wished, with all her heart, that Melody and her foal would make it.

Lou came back from Scott's that evening but she hardly spoke to Grandpa. As the next few days passed, the silences between them grew longer. There were no more arguments but the tension in the air was patent. Lou was determined to find their father. She rang round all the hotels and inns in the area to see if he'd been staying there, but apart from the time she was on the phone she avoided being in the house, spending her time on the yard with Ben and Ty, or going out with Scott.

For the first time in her life, Amy found herself almost looking forward to going to school each day; at least it meant she could escape from the atmosphere that pervaded Heartland. She longed to be able to do something about the growing rift between Grandpa and Lou but didn't know what she could do. Grandpa was adamant about not having their father at Heartland and Lou was equally determined to track him down.

On Friday afternoon, she was waiting expectantly when Amy got home from school. "I think I've found where Daddy was staying," she said, her eyes sparkling. "There was a Tim Fleming staying at a place called the River House Inn. He checked out on Sunday."

Amy stared at her. With each day that had passed, she had begun to think, with relief, that Lou wasn't going to be able to track their father down. "Was it definitely Daddy?" she stammered.

"I don't know," Lou said excitedly. "But I'm sure it must be. The name's right and they said he was tall with slightly greying hair and that he checked in there the day before Daddy visited here. They didn't know where he was going to next but they have got an address for him."

"Are … are you going to write to him again?" Amy asked.

"I already have," Lou replied. "I sent a letter off this afternoon. I told him that we were both desperate to see him." She must have seen the shock on Amy's face because she frowned. "I don't understand why you're looking like that. You told me that you wanted to find him. You told me that you'd *help* me."

Amy remembered her words the night that she and Scott had found Lou outside the cemetery. "I know," she said, trying to appease Lou. "And I do want you to find him, it's just..."

She broke off as Grandpa came into the room. The effect on Lou was immediate – a shutter seemed to fall across her face. "Well, I'll let you know if there's any news," she said abruptly to Amy, and then she turned and left the kitchen.

Amy didn't know what to say. The longer the argument went on, the less likely it looked that it would ever be resolved. She couldn't understand why they hadn't made up.

"Did ... did Lou tell you she thinks she's found where Daddy was staying?" she asked.

"No," Jack said, looking shocked.

"She's got hold of an address for him and she's already written to him again," Amy said.

Jack shook his head. There was a moment's silence between them.

"Grandpa," Amy whispered suddenly. "I don't want to see him."

Jack looked at her and then held out his arms. "Come here," he said.

Amy stepped forward and felt his arms close around her, warm and comforting.

"You know, you have to make that decision for yourself,

but whatever you decide," he said softly, "I'll always be here for you, no matter what."

Five minutes later, Amy made her way up the yard – she'd decided to distract herself for a while in an attempt to forget what Lou had told her. It was cold outside and she was glad of her warm jacket.

Seeing Ty coming out of the tack-room, she jogged up to meet him. "How's Melody been today?" she asked.

"A bit restless," Ty replied, "but I've walked her out several times and that seems to have calmed her down a bit."

Amy nodded. Scott had told them that it was likely that Melody would get livelier as her wound healed and her general condition improved. He'd also said that, all being well, they could start letting her out to graze for a few hours each day the following week.

"I'll go up and see her," Amy said.

Just then, Ben appeared, leading Red down from the training ring.

"How was he?" Ty called.

"Great," Ben replied, stopping and patting Red's powerful neck. "I just hope he'll be as good tomorrow."

"I bet he'll be totally brilliant," Amy said confidently. "Are you going to bath him?"

Ben glanced at the grey sky and shook his head. "It's too cold. I'll just wash his tail and give the rest of him a really good groom. I'll braid him in the morning." He clicked his tongue and carried on down the yard.

"The forecast says there's going to be snow in the next few days," Ty commented, as he and Amy continued to Melody's stall.

"I hope it holds off until after the show," Amy said, shivering.

Ty nodded.

They reached the back barn. Melody was looking out over her door. "Have you been restless today?" Amy said, stroking the mare's warm neck and looking at her churned-up bed. "I might take her for another walk," she decided out loud.

"Sure," Ty replied. "I'll sort her bed out while she's out of the stall."

Amy slipped Melody's halter on and led the mare down the drive. Melody's pregnant belly seemed bigger than ever. It was hard to believe that she still had another two weeks to go before the foal was due. She walked slowly and heavily and Amy noticed that her legs had filled up with fluid again.

"Poor girl," she said to the mare. "You'll be happier when you can go out and graze for a bit each day, won't you? Then the exercise can keep the swelling down."

She paused to let Melody nibble at the grass but to her surprise, the mare didn't seem that keen. She tore at a few strands and then lost interest.

Amy decided to take her back to her stall. She bumped

into Ben, who was carrying Red's tack. He frowned. "She looks close to foaling," he said.

Amy stopped Melody. "She can't be," she said anxiously. "She's still got two weeks to go."

"I'd say she's got no more than a week, maximum," Ben said. "Look at her hindquarters – all her muscles have slackened off. That normally only happens a few days before labour starts."

Feeling worried, Amy led Melody up to the barn and into her stall. What if Ben was right and Melody had her foal early? She would give Scott a call and see what he thought.

"Ben may be right," Scott said, when she got through to him and told him about Melody's condition. "But if she is about to foal it's not really too early. Mares rarely give birth on the day they're supposed to. Going into labour a couple of weeks either side of their due date is considered normal. In theory, the foal's health won't be at risk if it's born now."

"Will you come and see her?" Amy asked, feeling slightly reassured.

"I've got a really busy couple of days, I'm afraid," Scott said. "Why don't you see how it goes, and give me a ring if you get worried – otherwise I'll try and call in on Sunday."

There was a thick frost on the ground when Amy got up early the next morning. As she strode up the yard, she glanced at the grey sky. The clouds were heavy with snow.

She frowned, hoping that it would hold off at least until after the show.

Melody was walking restlessly round her stall. Amy went in and ran her hands over the mare's sides and hindquarters. The muscles felt soft.

"How is she?"

Amy turned and saw Ben standing by the door. "You're here early," she said in surprise.

"I didn't sleep that well," he replied. "I couldn't stop thinking about the show – and about seeing Mom."

"Well, Melody seems about the same as yesterday," Amy said, patting the chestnut mare. "She still seems restless." She frowned. "Perhaps I shouldn't come to the show after all. Maybe I should stay here."

"But you've got to come," Ben said quickly. "I need your support. The showground's only an hour away," he added. "Can't you ask your grandpa to keep an eye on Melody? If anything happens he can ring us on my mobile and we can come straight back."

Amy felt torn but she reluctantly agreed. "OK, if Grandpa doesn't mind."

Jack was preparing breakfast in the kitchen. He frowned as she came in. "You look worried, Amy," he said. "Is everything OK?"

Amy explained about Melody. "I'm really not sure about leaving her, but Ben really wants me to go to the show."

"You go," Grandpa said immediately. "I can keep an eye

on Melody. If there's any change, I'll ring you straight away." He seemed to see the uncertainty on Amy's face. "Don't worry about it, I might not have experienced many mares foaling but I've seen plenty of calvings. If the worst comes to the worst, I'll be able to hold the fort until Scott gets here."

Amy still felt torn but deep down she knew he was right. Grandpa had years of experience with farm animals. If anything happened, he would know what to do. "Thanks, Grandpa," she said. "I'll tell Ben I'll go with him."

Soraya arrived at eight-thirty. "Hello!" Amy called, coming out of Jake's stall.

"Hi," Soraya replied. She waved goodbye to her mom and ran up the yard to meet Amy. "So, what is there to do?" she asked, dumping her bag on the ground.

"A whole heap of stuff," Amy said. "There's the stalls on the yard to finish and all the horses to groom and then Melody to walk out. We're going to have to work quite hard because Ben is busy getting Red groomed and braided and we're leaving for the show at two o'clock."

Soraya immediately went to find a pitchfork and started helping Amy with Jake's bed. "Where's Ben right now?" she asked.

"In the barn," Amy replied. She thought about the way he had been hurrying through his chores that morning. "I think he's feeling a bit nervous."

Just then, Ben came to Jake's stall. "The stalls in the barn are done," he said to Amy. "Is it OK if I braid Red now?"

"Sure," Amy said. "Soraya and I will finish off the stalls down here."

"Great," Ben said, and jogged off.

"He does look nervous," Soraya commented to Amy in a low voice.

Amy nodded as she watched Ben disappear into the tack-room. She desperately hoped everything was going to go well for him that day – both in the ring *and* with his mom.

Chapter Nine

At two o'clock, Amy, Soraya and Ben loaded Red into the trailer and got into the pick-up. Grandpa came out of the house to wave them off.

"Good luck!" he called, as Ben started the engine.

Amy took one last glance towards the back barn and Melody's stall. She hated leaving her but knew she could trust Grandpa.

They reached the showground with an hour to spare before the class was due to start. Ben carefully steered the trailer through the horses and ponies milling around and found a quiet corner to park. "I'll go and sign in," he said, jumping out of the pick-up.

"Do you want us to get Red out for you?" Amy asked.

Ben nodded. "Yeah, thanks."

Soraya lowered the ramp while Amy went into the trailer.

As the ramp went down, Red let out a piercing whinny. The muscles on his neck were tense with excitement and he danced out of the trailer beside Amy, his head held high.

While Amy held him, Soraya removed the protective wraps from his legs and tail. He sidestepped excitedly.

"I think we'd better walk him around to calm him down," Amy said, seeing the damp patches of sweat darkening his neck.

"Do you think Ashley will be here?" Soraya asked as they put on Red's bridle.

"Probably," Amy said, pulling a face at the thought. Beautiful and wealthy, Ashley Grant was in their class at school. Her parents owned a hunter barn – Green Briar – and Ashley rode in shows nearly every weekend. The horses and ponies she rode were always expensive and very highly trained. She and Amy had often competed against each other in the Large Pony Hunter classes where, much to Ashley's disgust, Sundance had often carried off first prize.

However, as Amy and Soraya walked Red round the showground they didn't catch sight of Ashley or her family.

They had just begun to tack Red up when Ben returned with his number.

"Right," he said, "the classes are running on time so I should start working him in."

"He's quite excited," Soraya commented.

"He always is when he comes to a show," Ben said, patting Red's gleaming neck. "He loves them." He glanced down at his jeans. "I need to get changed too," he said. "Are you two OK looking after him for a bit longer?"

Amy nodded. "At your command – we'll do whatever you want."

Soraya giggled as Ben disappeared into the living quarters of his trailer. "You said it!"

Amy chucked Red's brushing boots at her friend. "Put these on!" she said with a grin. "And quit dreaming!"

Five minutes later, Ben came out of the trailer and Amy thought she was going to have to shut Soraya's mouth for her, it dropped open so far. Ben's jeans and barn jacket were gone and in their place were spotless white breeches, long leather boots and a beautifully cut, black show-jacket that hugged his broad shoulders. Even though Ben wasn't Amy's type, she had to admit that he looked totally amazing.

Seemingly oblivious to their reactions, Ben strode over to Red. "Thanks for tacking him up," he said, taking the reins.

"That's OK," Amy said, realizing that Soraya was incapable of speech.

Ben mounted. "I'll go and warm up," he said.

Amy and Soraya watched Ben ride off – Red prancing, his powerful muscles clearly defined under his glossy chestnut coat, Ben sitting effortlessly in the saddle. They looked perfect together.

"Wow!" Soraya breathed.

Amy grinned. "Come on, let's go and watch."

They found a space at the side of the training ring and

watched Ben start to school Red. The ring was busy, with horses and ponies cantering round in all directions and several trainers standing in the middle shouting out instructions. But Ben managed to find a reasonably quiet corner and began to work Red in.

Suddenly Soraya nudged Amy. "It's Ashley! Look!"

Amy glanced round. Ashley Grant was trotting into the ring on a beautiful bay hunter. Her long platinum-blonde hair was tied back in a single plait and her perfectly-tailored navy show-jacket accentuated her tall, slim figure. The only thing that marred the picture was the scowl on Ashley's face.

"Out of my way!" she snapped at a younger girl who was getting ready to jump one of the practice fences. Barging the bay hunter past the girl's grey pony, Ashley cantered towards the jump. The bay sailed over it, his dark coat gleaming like antique mahogany. Ashley smiled smugly as if she was aware of exactly how good she looked.

"How come she always has such lovely horses?" Soraya said. "It's totally unfair."

Amy nodded. She wouldn't have swapped Sundance for anything, but Ashley did get to ride the most wonderful horses. For a moment, Amy wished she had Sundance there so that she could at least attempt to wipe the self-satisfied smile off Ashley's face.

Just then, Ashley turned and saw them. "Oh no!" Amy groaned, under her breath, as Ashley turned her horse and began to canter towards them. "She's coming over."

Ashley stopped a couple of metres short of them. "What are you two doing here?" she demanded, as if they had no right to be at a show.

"What do you think?" Amy retorted.

"Well, you're obviously not competing," Ashley said, sweeping her green eyes disparagingly over their yard clothes. "Not even *you* would go into a ring looking like that, Amy."

Before Amy could reply, Ben came trotting over. "Can you take Red for me?" he said to Amy and Soraya. "I want to go and have a look at the course." Suddenly he seemed to notice Ashley. "Oh, sorry," he said quickly. "I didn't mean to interrupt."

"You haven't interrupted *anything*," Amy said pointedly.

"Of course we'll hold Red," Soraya said, jumping over the fence.

Ashley was looking at Ben. "Hi," she said, her lips curving into a smile. "I don't think we've met before. I'm Ashley Grant and you're..."

"Ben Stillman," Ben said, dismounting. "I work at Heartland." He held out his hand. "Nice to meet you, Ashley."

"And you," Ashley replied.

"Well, I'd better get on and walk the course," Ben said. "See you around."

"You can count on it," Ashley purred, giving him a little wave as he walked off.

Amy glanced at Soraya. She was biting her lip as she checked Red's girth.

"Ashley!" a voice bellowed. Ashley swung round. Her mother, Val Grant, was fast approaching through the crowds, a frown on her square-jawed face. "What are you doing?" she shouted. "You should be working Dreamtime in."

Ashley turned abruptly to Amy and Soraya. "See you, then," she said coldly, and cantered off.

"Can you believe Ashley!" Soraya exclaimed the second she was out of earshot. "Did you see how she was coming on to Ben?"

Amy nodded. "He didn't seem that interested, though," she said quickly.

"I guess." Soraya sighed. "I just wish he was interested in *me*."

After ten minutes, Ben came back from walking the course. "What's it like?" Amy asked.

"Not bad," Ben replied. He glanced at his watch.

"What time did your mom say she'd be here?" Amy asked, guessing what was on his mind

"Three-thirty," Ben said shortly. "Fifteen minutes ago."

"I'm sure she'll make it," Soraya said reassuringly. "She's probably just been held up."

"Or she's decided not to come," Ben said tersely. He swung himself back into the saddle. "I'd better keep Red moving – we're jumping fifth in the order." Without another word, he rode off.

Amy watched him trot back to the schooling area, his eyes

scanning the crowds. *Please let his mom get here in time*, she thought desperately.

The loudspeaker crackled and announced that the High Preliminary class was about to begin.

"Have we got a cloth to smarten Red up before he goes in?" Soraya asked suddenly.

Amy shook her head.

"I'll run back to the trailer and fetch one," Soraya said. She hurried off through the throngs of people and horses.

Amy looked around, willing Ben's mom to appear. In the training ring, Ben turned Red to a practice fence, but his concentration seemed to have gone and Red's forelegs clattered into the top rail. Glad of something to do, Amy slid between the fence boards, walked into the ring and put the fence up again.

"Thanks," Ben said, his face grim.

Dodging the cantering horses and shouting trainers, Amy went back to the fence. She saw Ben trying to canter Red in a figure of eight but the horse appeared to sense his owner's tension and threw his head up, fighting for the reins.

"And coming into the ring we have number 381," the loudspeaker announced.

"Ben!" Amy called. "You're next but two."

Ben rode Red towards her. Despite the cold, the chestnut was sweating. He tossed his head agitatedly.

Just then, Soraya appeared. "Here, I've got a cloth – I'll rub him down," she offered.

Ben's face relaxed for a second. "Thanks, Soraya," he said, as she started to rub the sweat marks away from Red's side.

"That's OK," Soraya said, smiling up at him.

Ben looked at them both. "And thank you both for coming today. It's good to have the support."

Amy heard a hard edge to his voice and realized he was thinking about his mom.

The loudspeaker crackled into life. "That was four faults for number 381, and now we have number 382 in the ring."

"You'd better go to the collecting ring," Amy said quickly.

Ben nodded and took up his reins.

As Red stepped forward, a voice called out, "Ben!"

Ben swung round abruptly. "Mom!" he exclaimed.

A woman was hurrying through the crowds towards them. The thick blonde hair that fell around her shoulders was exactly the same shade as Ben's and her blue eyes were the mirror image of his.

"I got held up on the way here," she gasped. "I thought I wasn't going to make it."

"Well, it wouldn't be the first time," Ben said, his voice suddenly cool. "I guess something came up at work, did it?"

"Work?" Judy Stillman said, looking at him in surprise. "I told you, I cancelled my meeting today. It was the snow. It's falling really heavily north of here."

"It's snowing!" Soraya exclaimed.

As Judy Stillman nodded, the loudspeaker made an

announcement. "Will number 384 come to the collecting ring, please – number 384."

"Ben! That's you!" Amy exclaimed.

Ben seemed to hesitate for a moment.

"Go on," his mom said. "We can talk later. I want to see you jump."

Amy saw some of the tension appear to leave Ben's face.

"Number 384!" the loudspeaker said.

Ben loosened his reins and Red plunged forward.

"Good luck!" Soraya called excitedly.

Ben turned in his saddle. "Thanks!" he shouted and then he cantered Red towards the collecting ring

"I'm Amy Fleming," Amy said to Mrs Stillman, realizing that they hadn't been introduced. "And this is my friend Soraya Martin."

"Judy Stillman," Ben's mom said. "It's nice to meet you both. I really thought I wasn't going to get here."

"We'd better go into the arena," Soraya said quickly. "Or we'll miss Ben's round."

They hurried to the viewing gallery of the indoor arena, found themselves some seats and sat down.

"Our first clear round," said the announcer, as the rider before Ben rode out of the arena to a round of applause. "And now we have number 384, Ben Stillman riding his own horse, What Luck."

"Here he is!" Amy exclaimed, grabbing Soraya's arm.

Ben came cantering into the arena on Red. He looked

calm and utterly focused, his lips moving inaudibly as he spoke quietly to his horse; Red seemed to mirror his rider's confidence. Amy crossed her fingers. They just *had* to do well.

The starting-bell rang out and Ben turned Red towards the first fence — a solid green and white oxer. Amy leant forward in her seat as the chestnut approached it smoothly. It felt as if she were riding the course herself — as if she could feel every stride Red was taking. Ben met the jump perfectly and Red soared over it, his forelegs snapping up neatly.

Then he was cantering towards the gate. He sailed over that and then over the upright, the wall, the red and blue double, another oxer and finally turned towards the treble. As he approached the line of three jumps, Amy held her breath. "Go on!" she breathed, knowing that if he could just clear this last combination then he would be into the jump-off. "Go on!"

Red took off over the first. He cleared it. He seemed to hesitate, but Ben sat down in the saddle and drove him on and in one stride he was over the second. Again he seemed to falter as he approached the third but Ben urged him on and Red responded. Taking two neat strides he cleared the final element.

"Yes!" Amy and Soraya exclaimed in delight, as the audience broke into a round of applause.

"And that's a clear round for Ben Stillman on What Luck," the announcer said over the clapping.

Amy was totally delighted. "He's in the jump-off!" she cried turning to Ben's mom.

Judy Stillman's eyes were shining with pride. "Wasn't he wonderful!"

Soraya jumped to her feet. "Let's go and find him!"

Quickly, they made their way outside. Ben had dismounted and was patting Red as if he was never going to stop.

Amy raced up to him. "Well done!" she gasped, patting the chestnut as well.

"Wasn't he totally brilliant?" Ben said to her, his eyes shining with happiness. "He didn't touch one."

Soraya reached them. "Way to go, Ben!" she cried.

Caught up in the moment, Ben embraced her. "We're in the jump-off, Soraya!" he exclaimed.

Amy saw the look of shock on her friend's face as Ben hugged her. However, it was quickly replaced by a smile of utter elation. "You were amazing!" Soraya gasped.

"Oh, Ben."

Hearing his mom's voice, Ben pulled away from Soraya and turned. Judy Stillman was standing behind him, her eyes shining with delighted tears. "I'm so proud of you," she said.

"Really?" Ben said, frowning suddenly.

Judy Stillman looked at him in surprise. "Of course! Why wouldn't I be? That was a wonderful round." She looked at him for a moment and then shook her head. "Ben, why do you insist in believing that I don't care?"

"Maybe because there hasn't been much evidence that you do," Ben said.

"That's not true, Ben," Judy protested.

"Isn't it?" Ben said, his voice suddenly cold. "I can't remember the last time you watched me ride."

"No!" Judy insisted. "I know the last eight years have been hard for you but you have to believe me, I've only ever done what I thought to be the best for you."

Ben laughed bitterly. "Including abandoning me at Lisa's?"

"Abandoning you?" Judy echoed. "But I came to see you every weekend."

"Yeah — at the start," Ben said.

Judy stepped towards him. "Did you think I didn't want to come?" she said intensely. "Ben, the reason I stopped visiting so often was because it seemed to upset you. You hardly ever spoke to me and just didn't seem to want me around. I talked it over with Lisa and we figured that it might be best if I gave you some space to settle down."

Amy saw the confusion in Ben's eyes. "But you always said it was your work." His voice, still angry, was now edged with uncertainty.

"That was just an excuse," Judy said. "I couldn't have just stopped coming without an explanation. I suppose it made it easier for me, that way…"

Ben looked confused. "I've always believed it was your work. I thought it meant more to you than I did."

Judy stared at him. "Ben, nothing has *ever* meant more to

me than you," she exclaimed. "I worked because I had nothing else in my life." Her voice suddenly shook. "Having you was the best thing that ever happened to me. You're my son and I love you."

There was a moment's silence. Slowly the confusion and hurt left Ben's face. "I didn't know, Mom," he said quietly. "Truly, I didn't."

Judy opened her arms. Ben hesitated for a brief second and then they embraced.

Amy and Soraya exchanged delighted grins.

Mother and son held each other for a long while. The moment was eventually broken by the sound of Red pawing at the ground.

"I think Red's saying he'd like some attention," Judy said, pulling back from Ben with a smile.

Ben nodded. "Getting jealous, boy?" he said, patting the big chestnut.

Red tossed his head.

"Come on, let's get you back to the trailer." Ben smiled. "You need a break before the next round."

There were ten horses in the jump-off. "So it's the fastest one who wins?" Judy asked, as Ben waited to go in.

"The quickest round with the least penalty points," Ben explained. "But I'm not going to hurry Red. He's still only young and I'd far rather he jumped a clear round than rushed it and knocked a load of fences down. There'll be plenty of time for him to build up speed when he's more experienced. I'm just pleased he's got into the jump-off."

Amy smiled at him. She hated seeing people pushing young horses before they were ready. It so often ended in the horses knocking jumps down and injuring or frightening themselves.

The horse before Ben came cantering out of the ring. "Good luck!" Amy and Soraya called, before going back to the gallery with Judy to find their seats.

Red tossed his head and snorted as he came into the ring and saw the jumps. He was obviously excited but Ben kept to his word – steadying him at the start before guiding him through a fast but careful clear round. When Red cantered out of the arena, his ears were pricked and his eyes confident.

"It was just the round I wanted," Ben said happily to the others when they'd hurried to congratulate him afterwards.

"It was fantastic!" Amy enthused, feeding Red a mint from her pocket.

And it was enough to earn Red a yellow ribbon for third place. Only two other horses jumped clear, the rest completing fast rounds but knocking fences down and so incurring penalty points. Amy, Soraya and Judy watched proudly as Ben rode Red into the ring to collect his ribbon. And as Ben cantered Red around the ring in a victory lap with the other six riders who had been placed, Amy was sure that she had never seen him look so pleased or confident.

She turned happily to Soraya. "What a perfect day!" she said.

As they untacked Red and got him ready for the journey home, Amy realized with a start how cold it had become. Her breath froze in the air, and as she fastened the wraps on Red's legs, a few flakes of snow drifted down from the sky and landed on the nylon straps.

"You'd better get going," Judy said, helping Ben put his tack away. "It's coming in from the north and the forecast is for it to get heavy later on."

"What are you going to do, Mom?" Ben asked.

"I was planning to head home," Judy said. "But looking at this weather, it might be best to find somewhere to stay round here for the night."

"You can stay at my place," Ben said quickly. "It's nothing special, but I have got a fold-out bed."

Judy smiled at him. "That sounds perfect. I'll follow you back."

It didn't take long to get Red loaded up, then Amy, Ben and Soraya climbed into the pick-up. It was starting to get dark now. "I hope we get back before too much snow falls," Amy said, looking up at the ominously thick clouds as Ben started the engine and the wipers swept across the windscreen.

"We haven't got too far to go," Ben said.

"And it's not snowing that hard yet," Soraya pointed out. She smiled at Ben. "Wasn't Red brilliant in the jump-off?"

As Ben and Soraya talked happily about Red, Amy watched the snowflakes falling through the dusk and thought about Melody. There had been no phone call from her grandpa which must mean that the mare was OK. Amy was relieved – the last thing they wanted was for Melody to go into labour if there was a heavy snowfall that night. The farm's winding drive could become impassable in deep snow.

As they drove north towards Heartland with Judy following, the snow started to fall more quickly and the drifts at the side of the roads became noticeably deeper. Eventually, they turned up the drive to the farm, the truck's wheels crunching into the frozen snow.

"Looks like we've got here just in time," Ben said.

The farmhouse door opened as they drove into the yard and Grandpa came out. He looked relieved to see them. "I was just about to ring you," he said. "I was worried about you getting back in this weather."

"It didn't start falling heavily until we were the best part of the way home," Amy said.

"Well, at least you're here now," Grandpa replied. "I've fed and rugged up the horses and there's a feed waiting for Red in his stall."

"Thanks, Grandpa," Amy said gratefully. "How's Melody?"

"Just fine." Grandpa turned to Soraya. "Your mom's been on the phone," he said. "I think you'd better ring her and let her know that you're back safely."

"Sure," Soraya said.

"I'll give you a lift home," Ben called as Soraya headed for the house. "It'll save your mom coming out."

Soraya smiled at him. "Oh, that would be great!"

Judy parked her car and got out. "This is Ben's mom," Amy explained to Grandpa. "She's staying with him tonight."

"Pleased to meet you." Judy smiled at Grandpa.

"Why don't you come and wait inside while Ben gets sorted out?" Grandpa offered.

Amy helped Ben unload Red and settle him into his stall. "I'll unbraid him for you," Amy offered. "You should head off before the snow gets any worse."

"Are you sure?" Ben said.

"Of course, no problem," she replied.

Ben went up to Red. "Bye, big fella," he said softly. "You were the best today." The chestnut snorted and nuzzled his head against his owner's chest. Ben rubbed his forehead and then turned and smiled at Amy. "Thanks for all your help."

"That's OK," Amy said. "See you tomorrow."

She waved goodbye as Soraya, Ben and his mom got into the pick-up, then went back to Red's stall. She had just taken out the first braid when Grandpa appeared with a mug of chicken soup. "Here," he said. "You must be starving."

"Thanks, Grandpa." Amy took it gratefully. She wrapped her fingers around the hot mug, savouring the warmth. It was impossible to take out braids with gloves on and her hands were freezing.

"So how was the show?" Grandpa asked.

Amy told him about Red's success and also about how Ben had made peace with his mom. "They finally seem to have put the past behind them," she grinned.

"That's good," Grandpa said quietly. "There's nothing worse than a family at odds." Amy heard the sadness in his voice and knew that he was thinking about Lou.

"How ... how's Lou been today?" she asked tentatively.

"She's been in her room most of the evening," Grandpa said. "Though she did come out and help me feed the horses when it started to snow."

"I'm glad," Amy said, feeling encouraged.

"Oh, she didn't speak to me." Grandpa sighed. "She hasn't said a word to me all day." He suddenly looked old and tired. "I'm going to make a start on dinner. Don't be out here too long."

Amy watched him go, wishing more than ever that there was something she could do to sort things out between him and Lou.

After unbraiding Red, Amy brushed the horse's mane out and then left him to a well-earned rest. She checked on all the other horses and then went down to the house. Lou made only a brief appearance at dinner-time and didn't even talk much to Amy, disappearing to her room again as soon as the plates were cleared. Amy sat with Grandpa in the warmth of the kitchen, watching TV while the snow continued to fall outside.

At ten o'clock, Amy reluctantly got up from her chair. "I'm going to check on Melody again," she said to Grandpa.

"I'm sure she'll be fine," Jack replied.

But Amy knew she wouldn't be happy unless she made sure. She pulled on her boots, thick coat and gloves and stepped outside. Snow swirled around her and a freezing wind bit into her cheeks. Shivering with cold, she fought her way through the drifts and up to the back barn.

Snow had piled up outside the doors and she had to fetch a shovel to clear it. With a great effort she heaved the door open and staggered into the quiet warmth of the barn. Sighing with relief, she shut the door behind her and felt for the light switch. As the lights lit up the darkness, she heard a few surprised snorts and rustles from the stalls.

Amy hurried down the aisle. "How are you, girl?" she said as she looked over Melody's door.

The words died on her lips. Melody was standing in her stall, her head down, her tail swishing. Damp patches of sweat stood out on her sides. Just then, a groan erupted from her and she sank to her knees. Amy caught sight of the beginnings of an opaque sac protruding from under Melody's tail and gasped. The mare was in labour!

Forgetting about the cold, Amy turned and raced back up the aisle and out of the barn. Stumbling and tripping she ran, half-blinded, through the snow.

"Grandpa!" she shouted, bursting into the kitchen. "Come quickly! Melody's having her foal!"

Chapter Ten

Grandpa was on his feet almost before the words had left Amy's mouth. "What? Now?" he exclaimed.

"Yes!" Amy gasped. "I could see the sac coming out of her."

Grandpa strode into the hall. "Lou!" he shouted. "It's an emergency." He began to pull on his coat and hat. "Where's the foaling kit, Amy?"

"In the tack-room," Amy said. "Shall I call Scott?"

Before Grandpa could answer, Lou came running into the kitchen. "What is it?" she asked, her eyes darting from Amy to Grandpa. "What's happened?"

"Melody's having her foal early," Grandpa said, going to the door. "Can you get in touch with Scott? I'm going up to the stall with Amy."

Lou grabbed the phone, her argument with Grandpa apparently forgotten in her desire to help. As she punched in the number, she asked, "Do you need me to do anything else?"

"Boil some water and bring it up to the stall," Grandpa said.

"Sure," Lou nodded as Grandpa strode outside.

Amy ran after him and together they fought their way through the blizzard, stopping only in the tack-room to collect the foaling kit.

"I hope this is going to be a regular foaling," Grandpa shouted as they stepped out into the wind and snow again. "Scott's going to find it hard to get through to us in this!"

Amy's heart was pounding so fast that she thought it was going to burst. "Come on, Grandpa! We have to hurry!" she said.

They reached the barn, its electric lights shining out like a beacon into the darkness. Amy ran down the aisle, hugging the foaling kit against her ribs. She could hear Grandpa behind her.

"She's still down!" she gasped, as Grandpa caught up with her at Melody's door.

The chestnut mare was lying in the straw, groaning as her sides heaved with a fresh contraction. Amy reached for the door bolt but Grandpa stopped her.

"We're best to stay out here," he said in a low voice. "Animals hate being disturbed when they're giving birth. If we go in it might upset her. Providing this is a regular labour, she's best left on her own."

Amy looked at Melody's hindquarters. More of the opaque bag — the amniotic membrane that covered the foal — could be seen under Melody's tail.

"The front hooves are out," Grandpa said, nodding towards the bag. "That's a good sign. The foal must be facing the right way."

Amy looked more closely and could see that he was right, two tiny hooves could be seen through the protective covering of the bag.

Melody's sides heaved again and the hooves and front legs slid out slightly more.

"Will we see the muzzle soon?" Amy asked.

Grandpa nodded. "It should be lying close against the front legs."

They watched as Melody continued to strain. Nothing happened. No muzzle appeared. Melody groaned.

"What's happening? Why's the head not coming?" Amy asked Grandpa anxiously.

Jack shook his head. "I don't know." A frown creased his forehead. "I hope it's not a malpresentation."

"What's that?" Amy asked quickly.

"It's when the foal isn't lying correctly," Jack explained. "The head is bent back either along the back or through the front legs. The foal gets stuck and can't be born. If it *is* a malpresentation Melody's going to need help."

Just then, the barn door opened and Lou hurried in with a covered bucket of water.

"Did you get through to Scott?" Grandpa asked.

"Yes," Lou replied, hurrying towards them, "but he says all the roads round here are blocked. He's already had another call-out that he couldn't get to."

Amy's eyes flew to his face. "What are we going to do, Grandpa?" she asked.

"I'm going to have to find out what's holding the birth up," Grandpa said quickly. He shrugged off his coat and began to empty the equipment out of the foaling bucket. "Can you find me the antiseptic soap, Amy?"

"What's wrong?" Lou asked, as Grandpa tipped some of the hot water into the bucket the foaling kit had been in and began to soap his hands and arms.

"Grandpa thinks the foal's got stuck," Amy said, so worried that she was hardly able to get the words out.

"But that's serious, isn't it?" Lou said.

Grandpa nodded and went into the stall. "It's OK, girl," he murmured to the mare. Hearing his footsteps, Melody looked round, her eyes wide and alarmed. As he approached, she began to try to struggle to her feet. Jack quickly backed off. "I think she's going to panic if I get too close," he said.

"I'll hold her," Amy said.

"She might not let you," Jack said. "She'll be in so much pain, she won't be thinking straight."

"Let me try," Amy said.

She saw Grandpa nod and went quietly into the stall.

Hearing the rustle of the straw, Melody's head shot into the air. "It's all right, girl, it's only me," Amy whispered.

Melody's head stayed high but she didn't try to stand up. Her ears flickered as Amy slowly approached. "Steady now," Amy murmured. She knelt down beside the mare's shoulder and began to move her fingers in quick, light circles over Melody's damp skin. Although she desperately wanted Grandpa to be able to find out what was wrong as soon as possible, she forced herself to control her movements.

"You've got to let us help you," Amy said softly as her hands worked. Gradually, she felt the mare start to relax. She slowly worked her fingers up Melody's neck towards her head and ears. As she worked, she moved round until she was kneeling in front of the mare. With a sigh, Melody dropped her muzzle into her lap.

"I think she'll be OK now," Amy said softly, glancing over her shoulder to where Lou and Grandpa stood by the door. They both looked pale and worried.

After scrubbing up again, Grandpa came quietly into the stall. Melody's eyes flickered uneasily but she didn't move. Trying to keep her own breathing regular because she knew it would help to calm the mare, Amy started to work in small circles on Melody's ears, her fingers stroking and soothing.

Grandpa approached quietly and then, crouching down in the straw, he inserted his arm inside the mare. He felt around for a few seconds and then swore.

"What's the matter, Grandpa?" Lou asked quickly.

"It's what I was worried about — the foal's head is bent back along its side," Grandpa said. He straightened up and went back out of the stall to wash his arm. "It's stuck fast in the birth canal."

"So what can we do?" Lou asked.

Grandpa's face was serious. "We need to turn the head. The problem is, it's so far back I don't think I can reach it." Amy saw the lines of worry etched along his face. "I'm going to have to ring Scott and see what he advises."

He hurried out of the barn. Amy looked at her sister. "Oh, Lou, what's going to happen?" she said.

"I don't know," Lou replied. She looked round. "Would it be a good idea if I put this straw down?" she asked. "I guess we should have the bed as clean as possible."

Amy nodded. "Do you want me to help?"

Lou's eyes flickered to Melody. "No, you stay there."

She worked quietly. Melody groaned again.

Feeling close to tears, Amy kissed the mare's face. "It's going to be OK," she whispered. "It is!"

They heard the barn door open and Grandpa appeared in the doorway. "What did Scott say?" Lou asked quickly.

Jack's face was serious. "We have to turn the foal round," he said.

"But I thought you said you couldn't reach it," Lou said.

"There isn't a choice," Jack said grimly. "If I can't reach the muzzle and turn it then both Melody and the foal will die."

Amy felt the blood rush from her face. "Die?" she whispered.

Jack nodded. "There's no chance of Scott getting through." He stripped off his coat and shirt again. "We have to get the foal out."

Amy heard him plunge his arm into the bucket again.

Melody sides contracted and Amy caught back a sob. *Please, please don't die*, she prayed, seeing the pain and distress in the mare's eyes.

Grandpa came into the stall and inserted his arm inside Melody again.

Forcing herself to focus, Amy worked on the mare's ears to help settle her. However, by now, Melody seemed to be past caring about Grandpa. Her breathing was hoarse and her neck was soaked in sweat.

For what seemed like an age, Jack struggled to get a purchase on the foal's head. "I can't get hold of it," he gasped. "If I could just hook my little finger in the corner of its mouth then maybe I could turn its head around, but I just can't reach."

"Keep trying, Grandpa," Lou said from outside the stall, her eyes scared.

Amy looked anxiously at Melody. The mare was starting to tire. What if they were too late?

"It's no use!" Grandpa said, after five minutes more.

"You can't give up!" Amy said.

"I don't think there's anything more I can do," Jack said desperately.

The next minute, Lou entered the stall. "You can do it, Grandpa," she urged, kneeling down beside him. "I know you can."

Jack took a deep breath and reached deep inside Melody again. His face contorted as he struggled to get hold of the foal's muzzle.

"Go on," Lou whispered.

Amy saw their grandpa's muscles bunch as he made one enormous effort. "Got it!" he gasped suddenly. "I've reached its mouth."

Amy caught her breath, hope flooding through her as Grandpa began to ease the foal's head round, inch by difficult inch. Was he going to be able to do it?

She bent her head to Melody's. "Please, please, please," she prayed frantically. "Please be OK."

"I've done it!" Grandpa exclaimed suddenly, collapsing back on to the straw.

"I can see its nose!" Lou gasped. The mare's sides heaved. "And here's its whole head!"

"Melody's tiring – she's going to need a hand," Grandpa said, struggling to his feet. "Lou, help me. We need to take the front legs just above the fetlock joints and pull as she pushes."

Lou did as he asked. Melody's sides shook in another contraction.

"Pull now!" Grandpa cried.

Amy saw their faces grimace with effort as they both

pulled hard. She had been holding her breath for so long now that she felt as if she was going to pass out.

Melody groaned.

"Here it comes!" Grandpa gasped. "Pull, Lou!"

Suddenly the foal's damp body slid out on to the straw.

Amy's heart almost stopped. "Is it dead?" she whispered, not knowing know whether to be relieved the foal was out or terrified by its stillness.

Being careful not to break the umbilical cord that attached the foal to Melody, Grandpa bent over to examine it. As he did so, Amy saw the foal's ears flicker and its head move.

"It's alive!" she cried, hot, sweet relief sweeping over her like a wave.

"Oh, Grandpa!" Lou exclaimed, flinging her arms round Jack.

He grinned happily. "Exhausted but alive," he said.

The tension in the stall dissolved. Grandpa stood with his arms round Lou while Amy stroked Melody's face and they watched the foal start to move in the straw. It was perfect. A tiny, chestnut replica of Melody with a white star on its forehead. First, its eyes blinked open and then it struggled on to its chest, its legs breaking through the membrane that still coated its body. As it struggled and kicked, the umbilical cord broke and the foal took its first breath of real air.

Grandpa fetched the iodine, cotton wool and antibiotic powder from the foaling kit and quickly dressed the umbilical stump while the foal was still lying down.

"It's a filly," he said, with a smile. "A little girl."

Suddenly, Amy felt Melody's nose move in her lap. Lifting her head, the exhausted mare looked round. Her ears pricked as she saw the foal. Amy hesitated for a moment and then edged away and joined Grandpa and Lou at the stall door.

Grandpa put his arm around her and together they watched mother and foal meet each other for the first time.

Melody struggled to her feet. Blowing down her nose, she sniffed all over the filly with loud snorts. The foal snorted back, her tiny nostrils opening wide, her bedraggled ears pricking clumsily. Melody nuzzled the foal's damp face and then began to lick its coat.

"They're bonding," Grandpa said softly.

Happy tears filled Amy's eyes. "I can't believe they both survived," she said. She turned to Grandpa. "And it's all because of you."

"Because of *all* of us," Jack said, looking at her and Lou.

"It was you that turned the foal, Grandpa," Lou said. "You were the one who wouldn't give up."

Amy saw an expression almost like regret cross Grandpa's face as he nodded. "I've always been stubborn," he said.

There was a pause. "Then I guess that makes two of us," Lou said softly, taking his hand. "I'm sorry about the way I've been behaving, Grandpa. I think I've always known, deep down, that you didn't mean to hurt me. But Daddy means so much to me and I couldn't bear the thought that he'd been here and yet you sent him away."

"I know," Grandpa said. "And I should never have done what I did." He looked at them both. "You two mean more to me than anything," he said. "I should never have put my own feelings before your happiness. Tim is your father and this is your home. You should be able to invite him here whenever you want." He paused. "Forgive me, Lou?"

"If you'll forgive *me*," Lou said, putting her arms round his neck and hugging him.

Amy let out a deep sigh of relief. It looked like the argument had finally been resolved.

"Poor Amy," Jack said, looking at her. "I guess the last week's been tough for you. You've really been caught in the middle, haven't you?"

"I'm just glad it's all sorted out," Amy said truthfully. She joined in with the embrace. "You two are the most stubborn people in the world."

Grandpa and Lou looked at each other and grinned.

"Well, apart from you," Lou said.

They all laughed. "Come on," Grandpa said as they separated. "Let's go inside. Melody and the foal will be just fine now."

"I think I'll stay for a little bit longer," Amy said, glancing at the foal. "Just until she gets up."

"OK," Grandpa said, nodding understandingly. "But don't try to help – it's important she learns to stand on her own."

"We'll see you later," Lou said.

Amy leant over the stall door and listened to the barn

door banging shut behind them. Feeling totally drained, she sank down in the straw and looked at the chestnut filly lying there, her long limbs so tiny but perfect, the white star gleaming on her forehead. There was only one more problem to be solved. "What shall we call you?" Amy whispered.

The little filly looked at her, her dark eyes bright.

Melody snorted softly and suddenly the foal began to make her first attempt to stand. Stretching out her long, spindly legs, she got halfway to her feet and then collapsed into the straw with a soft thud. Amy longed to help her but she knew Grandpa was right – it was a lesson the foal had to learn on her own.

With a toss of her head, the filly tried again. Her legs stretched and braced and then with a heave she was on her feet. She wobbled for a second and then fell over.

"Come on," Amy urged under her breath. "You can do it!"

The filly rested in the straw for a few minutes and then Melody nudged her side. Out came the foal's legs again. She paused, a look of determination on her face and then she struggled into a stand. Her legs braced, she swayed a little, but this time she stayed on her feet. For a few moments, she just stood there, wobbling slightly. Then with a quick wag of her fluffy tail, she took an uncertain step forward and thrust her muzzle under Melody's belly.

Melody nuzzled her flank and the filly began to feed.

Amy smiled and leant her head back against the wall,

shutting her eyes. It had been a long day but, at last, everything was OK.

Several hours later, Amy awoke with a start. Where was she? She looked round and everything came flooding back. Melody and the foal were safe. They were lying in the straw, the foal's head resting against Melody's side. Glancing at her watch, Amy saw that it was six o'clock. She'd been in the stall all night.

Feeling stiff, she got slowly to her feet. The foal's eyes blinked open and she raised her head, her tiny ears twitching.

Amy stood still. "It's all right," she murmured. "Stay there."

The foal looked at her for a long moment and then, with a sigh, she dropped her muzzle and shut her eyes again.

Amy crept out of the stall and shut the door as quietly as she could. There would be plenty of time to get to know the foal later in the day – right now she knew that Melody and her baby needed to rest. Stretching her cramped muscles, she walked to the barn door. Then, taking hold of the handle, she braced herself for the blizzard outside. However, as she pushed it open she heard nothing but silence.

As she stepped out, her boots crunched in the deep snow. The blizzard had stopped. The air was still and, in the night sky above, a tapestry of stars glittered. Amy shut the door and took a deep breath of the clear, cold air. Silence surrounded her – intense, deep and peaceful.

Amy looked around at the buildings and fields of Heartland spread out before her. Everything was covered in a blanket of thick snow. As she looked towards the east, she saw the first pale-grey glimmers of daybreak creeping across the dark sky and suddenly she knew what Melody's filly should be called.

"Daybreak," she whispered. For a new beginning, and the start of a new life.

Read More about

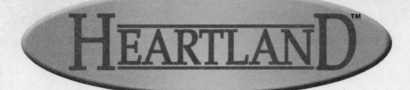

Healing horses, healing hearts. . .

LAUREN BROOKE
HEARTLAND

Coming Home

Healing horses, healing hearts. . .

LAUREN BROOKE
HEARTLAND

After the Storm